# A Neighborly Killing

## A Regan McHenry Real Estate Mystery

## Nancy Lynn Jarvis

Good Read Mysteries
An imprint of Good Read Publishers

This is a work of fiction. Names, characters, places, and incidents are either
products of the author's imagination or are used fictitiously.
Any resemblance to actual events, locales, or persons, living or dead, is
entirely coincidental.

**Good Read
Mysteries**

Good Read Mysteries © is a registered trademark of Good Read Publishers
301 Azalea Lane, Santa Cruz, California, 95060

Copyright © April 2016 by Nancy Kille

Library of Congress Control Number: 2016934877
ISBN: 978-0-9973667-0-9

Printed in the United States of America

www.GoodReadMysteries.com

Books are available at special quantity discounts through the website.

Sometimes inspiration for a story comes like a gunshot
in the middle of the night.

## Acknowledgments

Acknowledgments always start with Craig without whom I couldn't do this. He deals with computers and saves me from having to throw them against a wall. He's also my go-to guy for initial editing, book cover implementation, and encouragement, and most importantly, it's his eyes I see when I'm writing about Tom's blue eyes.

Once again, thanks to Morgan Rankin for her great editing.

# A Neighborly Killing

Nancy Lynn Jarvis

*It's unnerving to be awakened by gunfire, but when it's in your backyard, that's hardly something you can ignore. When a body is the result of what shocked you out of sleep, you don't get over it easily. And when it turns out the dead man is your next door neighbor, well, that calls for some serious questioning. At least that's the way I see it.*

*Regan McHenry*

Regan was one more flutter of eyelashes away from sleep. When she startled awake, her eyes wide open, she didn't trust what she had heard. She thought she might have imagined the sound in the split second before sleep came.

Tom, lying in bed next to her, flinched slightly with the second report.

"What was that?" she asked, rolling in his direction and putting her hand lightly against his back.

"A gunshot. A rifle shot." His voice was barely louder than a whisper, but it held no hint of sleepy haze.

She pushed an elbow under her and propped herself up so she could see over his shoulder to the outside. After promising El Niño rains in January, the skies had dried and temperatures hit record highs, leaving California still in a drought on this leap year last night of February. A rainfall Miracle March looked possible, though, and their house, at sixteen-hundred feet elevation on the windward side of the Santa Cruz Mountains, was under promising clouds, teasing that they might produce rain. She couldn't see anything clearly in the diffused light of their mist-filled cloud cover except the bricks of their patio which glistened with moisture.

"Do you think it's pig hunters?"

It had been several years since Bonny Doon had an outbreak of wild pigs. That episode was ended by experienced pig hunters who asked only for the meat they killed in exchange for ridding the countryside of the destructive beasts.

"Not on a night like this and not so near houses. The pig hunters gave notice a few days before they started hunting, too, so no one would be concerned when they heard shots, and they only hunted right after nightfall and right before dawn. Besides, I haven't heard anyone complain about pigs lately. Have you?"

"No, I haven't …"

Two more shots rang out in rapid succession, the second shot sounding before the echo of the first ceased.

Tom sat bolt-upright in bed. "Those blasts were close, I bet not more than thirty yards away." He swung his long legs to the floor. "Whoever is shooting, they're moving in our direction and getting awfully close."

Regan usually loved the glass wall on the back side of their house which provided wonderful views over Monterey Bay and the Pacific Ocean. Tonight that feature made her feel exposed and vulnerable. As the gunshots came closer, she would have happily traded the view for substantial bullet-stopping walls.

Tom was out of bed, robe-less, and searching for his rubber-soled slippers. As soon as he found them and wiggled his feet into them, he reached for the putter he had stowed between his nightstand and the window. He gripped it tightly in one hand as he stood at the bedside sliding door, open a couple of inches for fresh air, and peered into the night.

Regan's tone was apprehensive. "You're not going to …"

"I can make out a light," he said in a soft voice. "It's blurred and small; could be from a flashlight. It's close, coming from the hillside below our patio and moving toward us."

Regan thought she could see a faintly brightening patch beyond the patio's edge, too.

"I want you away from the windows." Tom barked a command at her in a husky whisper, "Go! Open the garage door and get in your car. Be ready to leave."

"No. Not unless you come with me."

The light outside stopped moving. There was another shot, but it sounded different from the previous shots. It lacked the power and resonant sound of rifle fire and was just a pop. The hillside light moved downhill a few feet and stopped.

As they waited for what would come next, Regan forgot to breathe. She strained to hear any sounds through the narrow door opening.

Was she imagining it or were there voices outside? Tom cocked his head. She wasn't imagining; he heard something, too. The voices grew loud enough to fill the night. Words reached Regan's and Tom's ears, but they were shouted and full of emotion … and impossible to understand.

After a time, the voices ceased and all grew quiet again as the night was suddenly more brightly illuminated than it had been. The silence was rent once more, first by a long wailing cry, and then by another pop. The sky darkened abruptly, the small light wavered, and after a couple of seconds, pointed upward like a wispy beacon.

Regan slipped out of bed and pressed against the wall by their headboard with zeal, as if proximity to wood framing covered in sheetrock might offer some protection from a bullet.

"Go! Now!" Tom snapped, but she made no movement to do what he ordered.

Regan and Tom froze into tense poses, still and listening. The night remained silent. The bedroom wall clock, ticking off seconds with earsplitting abandon, was the only sound they heard.

After listening to the oppressive quiet outside for a good two-minute interval, Tom instructed, "Stay where you are then, if you insist, but be ready to call 9-1-1 if you hear anything ... anything ... and if you do — I mean it — leave, get out of here."

He slid the door open fully before she could protest, and pushed the screen slider open enough to squeeze through, crouching low as he cleared the door. He rested the putter on his shoulder and moved stealthily toward the edge of the patio, stopped there, slowly raised his head to peer over the low brick wall, and strained to see into the darkness. Then with a sudden move he vaulted over the wall. He stayed bent low, and using the golf club like a ski pole to aid his balance, he began descending the steepening slope that separated the civilization of their patio from the woodlands below. He disappeared from Regan's view.

The tension Regan felt seemed to stretch time; even so, she didn't have to wait long to see Tom reappear. He had added a flashlight to what he was carrying and moved rapidly uphill. The features of his face, lit from below by the flashlight, looked haunted.

"Call 9-1-1. Tell them I found … I can't be sure, but I think it's our neighbor, Paul."

"Is he dead?" Regan asked even though she knew what his answer would be.

"Most definitely."

Dave, though still on the Santa Cruz Police Department payroll, was not usually called on for middle of the night duty. He was grumpy as he joined the officer interviewing Regan and Tom in their living room. It was a little after 2:00 a.m. He could have used either strong coffee or more sleep. He had lost an eye in a line-of-duty-shootout years before and wore a convincing artificial replacement that perfectly mimicked his sighted eye. Tonight it looked as drowsy as he did.

"I have to be on TV pretty regularly and I don't wear makeup — wouldn't be manly or in keeping with my being with the police force to wear makeup — so I need my beauty sleep, and, thanks to you," he aimed his complaint at Regan, "I'm not getting any tonight, am I?"

"Don't blame me," she answered defensively, "I called the police, not you."

He twisted his face into a "how dense you are" kind of smirk. "They probably heard your name, knew how your meddling has a way of putting you in the midst of murder investigations, and how I'm your friend and the one who always has to set things straight with the police when you make a mess, and just assumed ..."

"Actually, Officer Everett, I'm the one who had you called," the policeman offered. "And I didn't know y'all were friends or that you had a history," he drawled with a soft southern tempo more suited to Tennessee than Santa Cruz, California.

"Media already picked up on this ... situation. If you didn't pass them on the way in, it's only because their camera crew must have gotten lost on the way up here. Maybe someone new to the area like I am accidently sent them to Ben Lomond instead of Bonny Doon," he winked at Regan. "Both those locations sound the same to me, both kinda like places in Scotland.

"Even so, it's just a matter of time 'til they figure it out. They'll be clamorin' for a comment from our Police Ombudsman, which is you, Officer Everett. I kinda thought you'd like a heads-up; wouldn't like getting blindsided by some hotshot news reporter with a mic and a camera on your way to work tomorrow morning. But I just figured someone would fill you in with as much as we know so far. I didn't think anyone would tell you to get out of bed and come on up here."

"Oh, Dave, no one did, did they? You came on your own," Regan cooed. "You sacrificed your cozy bed to make sure we're OK."

Dave ignored her, concentrating instead on the notes the police officer handed him. He scanned quickly and handed them back.

"You found the body, Tom?" His question and the next words from him were more rhetorical than questioning and delivered rapidly. "You went out into the woods in the middle of the night after a gunshot in close proximity to your house woke you and Regan up, armed with your trusty putter? Is that right? And after you found the body, you picked up the flashlight near it so you could take a good look at the guy, thought he might be your neighbor from down the road, and used the flashlight to make it easier to see climbing up the hill. Is that about right?"

"I shouldn't have picked up the flashlight, should I, even though it was away from the body and wedged into the Vinca plants?" Tom sounded mildly embarrassed.

"No, you shouldn't have. You shouldn't have done any part of what you did. See now, I can understand if it was Regan doing something reckless and stupid — I'd almost expect it of her — but I thought I could count on you to be the reasonable one in this," he waved his hand in their direction, "duo. For all you knew, somebody just popped your neighbor and could have been lurking, ready to do the same thing to you if you got too close to him. You're lucky we aren't investigating a double homicide."

Tom nodded sheepishly. "In retrospect I can see that, but at the time I was pumping adrenaline." His eyes softened for the first time since he awoke and he tried to diffuse Dave's annoyance with humor. "Besides, I was carrying my lucky putter to defend myself — had it by my bedside ready for tomorrow's — today's — big round of golf — so nothing bad could have happened to me."

Dave's response was more wistful than judgmental.

"Yeah, right. Hormones and bravado. That's how I lost my eye in that shootout. Law enforcement guys like me are trained not to stick our necks out, but in the heat of the moment … adrenalin working instead of my brain … So now that's why I'm gonna' be wearing this prosthetic eye the rest of my life and why I'm a media guy now instead of a regular cop. Tom, you took a big chance."

"And an excellent prosthetic it is, Officer Everett, the way it tracks with your real eye," the young police officer empathized before getting the conversation back on track. "Sir, Ma'am, you were fixin' to tell me about the gunshot you heard."

"Gunshots. There were four gunshots that sounded like rifle fire and then one pistol shot, and after a long pause and what sounded like an argument, another pistol shot." Tom's statement and his words were clear and precise.

"Six shots?" the policeman frowned.

"That's right. Four and two."

"And you're sure about that?"

Regan confirmed what Tom said. "I heard them, too. And the voices." Regan looked at Tom for confirmation.

He nodded in agreement. "Our slider was open a few inches so we got some sound from outside. I couldn't be one-hundred percent certain, but it sounded to me like there were two voices outside, agitated voices. They certainly could have been arguing."

Regan shuddered as she spoke. "Then there was that quiet and then that terrible scream — it almost didn't seem human — and then the final gunshot."

"Ahh," the policeman wiped his upper lip with his finger,

"could I talk to you for a minute, Officer Everett? In the kitchen."

"Problem?" Dave quizzed the officer.

The officer ignored Dave's question. He swiftly rose to his feet. "Excuse us, please, ma'am, sir," he said politely as he started toward Regan and Tom's kitchen.

Dave raised his eyebrows toward Regan and then silently followed the officer.

"Why the need for privacy?" Tom asked when he and Regan were alone.

She put a hand on his, raised a finger in admonition and mouthed a soft, "Shh."

They listened intently, trying to eavesdrop, but couldn't make out the kitchen conversation until Dave's voice became sufficiently animated. "Of course they're reliable witnesses, both of them, her maybe even more than him. And if they agree, I'd say rock solid. So Tom took the flashlight. He would have admitted it if he tampered with anything else, especially a weapon. And as for wanting publicity — good grief — having a body found outside their house, that's the last kind of publicity they'd want."

🏠🏠🏠🏠🏠🏠🏠🏠🏠🏠🏠

Tom didn't let a little thing like only getting a couple of hours sleep and a dead neighbor keep him from his Wednesday morning golf outing. He and his foursome had an 8:30 a.m. tee time at the Pasatiempo Golf Course, and with commute traffic to consider and breakfast to be eaten at the clubhouse before the round, he kissed Regan goodbye in the dawning morning just before 7:30.

Regan curled up in front of the TV in her robe — an upgrade from her usual pajamas-only routine — in deference to the forensic team that was still wandering around their hillside. She had given up trying to sleep as soon as Tom left their bed. He may have been nonplussed by a so recently discovered body just yards from their home, but she wasn't, even after the coroner had come and gone with the remains.

She clicked on the eight o'clock local news broadcast expecting to see Dave detailing the night's grisly find as the lead story, but with a shooting in Salinas overnight and a grassfire near Watsonville that had everyone on edge, Dave only made the number three story spot.

He sported a blue, green, and white shirt, still Hawaiian in theme in keeping with his trademark look, but a subdued piece of clothing for him. He could have used some of the stage make-up he forswore; he looked as tired as she felt.

"Residents in normally quiet Bonny Doon were awakened last night by gunfire," the reporter announced from off camera, keeping the focus on Dave. Regan counted a small blessing: their names and address hadn't been included by the reporter. She'd bet money that omission was Dave's doing and she planned to say thanks to him with a proper note attached to a six-pack of his favorite beer. "Santa Cruz Police Ombudsman Dave Everett has the details."

"The investigation is still in the preliminary stages, but at this time the coroner does not believe foul play was involved in the death. It appears that the deceased was the victim of a single self-inflicted gunshot wound."

"What?" Regan was so startled by Dave's statement that she questioned his image on the TV screen out loud, "What about the shots we heard, and the voices?"

"The deceased, a male in his mid-forties, has been positively identified; however, his name is being withheld pending notification of his family."

The reporter was clearly disappointed by Dave's brevity and the lack of titillating details being offered. He finished using his best hard-driving reporter technique. "There are some unexplained circumstances surrounding the death, aren't there, Officer Everett?"

Dave raised his eyebrows ever so slightly and tilted his head just a bit, aiming a benign look at the persistent reporter. "Other than the fact that the apparent suicide took place near a neighbor's house rather than on the victim's property, no, nothing seems to be unusual in this sad case."

Regan debated calling Tom immediately, but decided to give him a chance to enjoy his round of golf before she told him Dave had just gone public with a big whopper about what happened last night.

It was Wednesday, technically Regan's day off, but as soon as she showered and had breakfast, dressed in leggings, boots, and a comfy oversized sweater — her way of emphasizing that she wasn't heading to work to work — she drove to their real estate office.

What Dave said on TV wasn't what happened. Being yards away from murder was horrific, death at another's hand always was, but a dishonest death — murder being touted as a suicide — somehow that was worse. Was Dave aware of the discrepancies between what he said occurred and what she and Tom experienced? He must be. There must be an explanation for why he misled the public and eventually he would share it ... unless there wasn't ... or he couldn't.

Regan's drive was consumed with questions and wondering. If she was going to make any sense out of what happened the night before, she needed some background information on their dead neighbor. His property had been for sale on and off for nearly half a decade and was once briefly listed with Kiley and Associates, the company she and Tom owned. They would have kept records of the listing.

Regan wanted to see the original file and read the listing agent's notes, the real-time ones, not the computerized transcription of them. Information could sometimes be ascertained by noting the slant of the listing agent's handwriting, the size of it and the pressure the pen exerted on paper. If there were doodles, so much the better. She might be able to glean some of the emotion the agent felt while writing by hand, details that would be lost in transcription. Seeing the original file wouldn't be a substitute for speaking to the principles, but it would be a starting point and might offer other information, as well.

The coffee she picked up from nearby Kelly's Bakery hadn't even cooled before she was at her desk thumbing through the retrieved file. First up was the listing agreement. Listing agent: Gretchen Howell. Owner: Pablo Valentino. Seeing the owner's name gave her momentary pause. She had always known him as Paul Valentine. He had Anglicized his name, if not officially, for presentation to people he knew locally. When Regan got to the listing price, $1,030,000, she stopped cold. She leaned back in her chair and took a long sip of coffee.

Real estate was a curious business. Individual agents were independent contractors and as such not under the direct supervision of their broker. Tom was the broker of record for Kiley and Associates so his neck would share the chopping block with an agent who erred, but he could only put systems in place and require that agents abide by company regulations. He couldn't tell them how to conduct many aspects of their business. Agents could take a listing and attempt to sell property for the price the owner and they agreed to without consulting the broker.

Regan recalled seeing Paul Valentine's property when Gretchen Howell listed it and remembered that the list price was much more than it was worth.

After the office tour, Regan put the small house on her 'D for dog' list, not because it was a mess, but because it was so overpriced for its size. D list placement meant she wouldn't waste her time showing the property to her buyers, so she quickly forgot about it.

A fast flip though the listing packet revealed Gretchen had invested a lot of money in advertising. Exclamation points after some of the advertising charges she had recorded made it clear she was aware of what Paul Valentine's listing was costing her, but then she asked Tom to release the seller from the listing contract well before the six-month term was up. Whose idea was that? Surely, given the quantity of pricey ads she ran, the seller had no grievances about Gretchen's marketing efforts. Even if he did, after investing so much money, Gretchen should have insisted on keeping the listing active, hoping it would generate new clients for her so she could recoup some of her investment, even without a sale.

The folder's contents were interesting, and as she hoped, reading between the lines was revealing. As she read, Regan scribbled questions on a notepad. She'd ask Gretchen about the listing when time and privacy permitted.

After returning the folder to the file drawer, Regan entered the property address on the computer to bring up its public listing history. What she saw warranted another slug of coffee. Gretchen, it seemed, had listed the house for a more realistic price than other agents before or after her.

Pablo Valentino, aka Paul Valentine, was an occasional for sale by owner, FISBOs in real estate jargon, but mostly he had used out-of-area agents to market his property. First up had been an agent from the central valley who listed the property for $1,200,000. When his six-month contract expired, a Los Gatos agent was hired who sought $1,099,999 for what he billed as a fifty-acre working horse ranch ready for timber harvest and division into two parcels. He had relisted the property two more times, once for six months and then for a year, never bringing the price below $1,049,999. She wondered how much marketing he had done to earn such a lengthy listing and added that question to her list.

Regan noted the agent's affinity for 9s. More importantly, she also noted that he seemed unaware that the parcel's zoning made it too small for division, that the County wouldn't be thrilled about a timber harvest, and that local anti-harvest activist Taylor Bingham and her cronies would fight a harvest tooth and nail if the County didn't, and that horses were no longer welcome in Paul's area of Bonny Doon. Those were all facts a good local listing agent would have known.

Following the two-and-a-half-year tie-up of his property, Paul made his second attempt at selling real estate as a For Sale by Owner and put the asking price back at $1,300,000. His increased price spoke volumes. It seemed neighbor Paul/Pablo wasn't particularly motivated to sell, but if he didn't want to, why bother to list his property at all, even as a FISBO? That question warranted another note on her pad.

Regan read her dead neighbor's marketing description. He had dropped the parcel split pledge, but still assured potential buyers that the property was zoned for a lucrative timber harvest and suitable for horse boarding.

Evidently Paul believed he had solved the horse dilemma because it was during his second tenure as a FISBO that the now infamous table and chairs appeared on his house website and he began bragging to his neighbors about how he beat *the man*.

Like Regan and Tom's parcel, in earlier years Paul's land had been zoned to permit horses, but they were now discouraged. A nearby creek had been added to the runoff collection area for town water and the County wanted to protect the water source from contaminates by disallowing any development. Regan had been told by one county planning employee that if their house hadn't been built years before, it couldn't be built today. The zealous staff member might have been puffing in stating his opinion, but disgruntled locals often accused the County of blocking them from using their property as they saw fit.

That must have been what Paul thought after he advertised horse boarding as one of his property's uses. County inspectors descended on him telling him that in order to have horses he must have a covered area to protect them from rain and sun or he could be charged with animal cruelty. But then they denied him permits to build the mandated structure. After he fumed for a while, Paul came up with an unusual solution.

Since there were no county rules regulating art, he built an outrageously large dining set and dubbed it a garden sculpture. Paul's artwork, clearly visible to anyone driving on Empire Grade, the ridge road running up from town and passing next to his property, was a twenty-foot square table supported at the corners by weighty redwood poles which held the tabletop eighteen feet above the ground. He fabricated two gargantuan chairs, as well. One was toppled as if a gigantic dinner guest had overindulged in spirits and had tilted back too far and fallen over. Its disrupted seat became the front wall of a tack room — carefully sized to be under the number of square feet that would require a permit — hidden from view from the road by the chair's angle.

The other chair was more conventionally placed under the table, although slightly askew, like it had been left that way by the drunkard's companion as he got up to help his fallen friend. Paul topped his whimsical magnum opus with a yard-tall dark blue ceramic vase filled to overflowing with a rainbow-bright bouquet of painted wooden flowers.

During the summer, horses dwarfed by the dining set stood in the shade of the table and upright chair. During winter months when rain was expected, Paul used the vase to anchor a massive and sturdy tarp patterned with red and white checks so it resembled an oilcloth tablecloth which he unfurled and let fall over the tabletop edges to the ground. Once he secured the grommet-rings on its perimeter with tent stakes, his horses had a cozy protected enclosure to keep them dry during winter storms.

Residents of Bonny Doon gave the structures mixed reviews. Some property rights advocates said what Paul had done was very 'Bonny Doon' and liked his stance against the County. Others said his art wasn't even an original idea, photos of a similar, if far less ambitious, table and chairs having been posted on the internet some years before he built his. Two things were certain, though: people driving up Empire Grade to the Crest Ranch for their Christmas trees stopped in droves to photograph the roadside feature, and no buyers came forward as a result of his efforts.

Regan thought she remembered a third consequence of the garden art: there was some dust-up and a county planner had been fired because of it. She made a note to research that before she continued looking up recent listing iterations of Paul's property.

Gretchen was next up in the timeline. After her listing ended, Paul went back to his FISBO ways for a few months and then listed the property with another out-of-area broker for $1,050,000 just two weeks before he died.

The property had been continuously offered for sale with agents or by Paul except for two brief off-the-market times. Regan remembered one of the time-outs because he had taken down all real estate and for sale signs and replaced them with signage of a quite different nature. His new sign at the property entrance announced Sunday morning church services and invited visitors to attend the outdoor events at his house.

The invitation sign remained in place during the summer but disappeared before Labor Day. She had never attended and didn't know what size congregation assembled for the services. All she knew was that the music that accompanied Paul's church gatherings stopped after he took down his welcome sign. Whether that was because he lost interest or his religious beliefs, whether congregants were no longer interested in attending, or whether Paul miscalculated the advantages — tax or emotional — of turning his property into a religious retreat every seventh day was unclear. She scribbled a note on her pad about it.

The final time-out had occurred just before the last listing. Paul had been FISBOing again, but removed his phone number and the property address on his most recent website and took down the signs with contact information that had graced his property entrance before listing with the latest agent. Regan scribbled the new listing agent's phone number on her notepad. He warranted a phone call, too.

She glanced at the clock in her office. It was past 9:30, early enough that Dave wouldn't have taken a coffee break yet, but late enough that he would soon be thinking about it. She turned off her computer, tossed her purse on her shoulder, and headed toward the office back door. Their receptionist was just arriving for the day as she was leaving.

"Hi, Regan. Are you working today? It's Wednesday, you know."

"No, Amanda. I'm not really here. I just wanted to have a quick look at a file."

"Did you hear the news? Your friend Dave was on TV this morning; somebody in Bonny Doon committed suicide last night, I guess kind of spectacularly, I mean, not quietly at home."

"Really?" Regan tried for a credibly surprised reaction. "I'll have to ask him about that," she parried as she left the building.

Asking Dave about the neighborhood suicide — the alleged suicide — was exactly what she intended to do.

Her first stop was at Iveta on Delaware Street. Regan knew Dave's tongue had on occasion been loosened by food and that scones were one of the best lubricants available. If cinnamon raisin scones were on Iveta's morning menu and if they were still warm, he'd be talking in no time.

🏠🏠🏠🏠🏠🏠🏠🏠🏠🏠🏠🏠

Regan was disappointed that the daily scone was boysenberry, but she didn't need to be. Dave was enthusiastic about the contents of the coffee break bag she brought him. He sat with feet propped up on his desk, studying his fingers to be certain that he had licked off every errant drop of boysenberry before he stuffed his hand into the open bag to retrieve another scone.

Regan appeared to be as focused on her scone as Dave was on his, but she nibbled with an ulterior motive. She wanted Dave to explain what he said on the morning news broadcast, and thus far, having guessed the dual purpose of her visit, he hadn't, savoring making her wait for information almost as much as he was enjoying his boysenberry scones.

Dave finally broke his silence as he returned his feet to the floor. "Hey, well thanks for these. They definitely make up for me having to get up in the middle of the night. I hate to eat and run, but I have a lot to do this morning so I'm going to kick you out and get back to work ..."

Regan had no choice; she had to leave quietly or come clean. "You know I'm not here just because we're friends enjoying a coffee break together."

The grin that spread across his face was immense. In their on-going game of one-upmanship, he had just scored a point.

"I figured you saw me on TV this morning and that what I said would eat at you. I knew it was just a matter of time before you got meddlesome."

"Of course I saw your interview. I couldn't believe my ears. The coroner doesn't really think our neighbor was a suicide, does he?"

"The investigation is still in the preliminary stages ..."

"Stop it! I'm not that reporter. What about the argument Tom and I heard? You don't think we imagined that, do you?"

"No, I don't." Dave shook his head. "The ground was moist overnight so the forensic team was able to find footprint impressions. Tom didn't help the crime scene tromping on it like he did, but he has big feet and was wearing slippers without much pattern on the soles. The team identified another set of footprints besides his from someone with smaller feet than Tom has. We know your neighbor wasn't alone."

"So our neighbor *was* shot." Regan sounded triumphant.

Dave scrunched the features of his face into a tight scowl. "Probably not. Tests are still being done, but based on the preliminary findings from the gunshot residue found on your neighbor's hands, it looks like he fired both the rifle near his body and the handgun that killed him, which he still clutched in his cold dead fingers, by the way."

Dave watched Regan closely hoping his description of her neighbor's hand would elicit a reaction, but she showed no sign if it did. Her mind was moving too quickly to linger on his words.

"If he had gunshot residue on his hands, that only proves

he fired both the rifle and the handgun. Couldn't another gun have been used to kill him?"

"First impression is that there wasn't another gun used. Ballistics will prove if the bullet that killed him came from the handgun he was holding for sure, but last I heard the bullet that killed him looks like a match for his handgun.

"And, not that I'd expect an amateur sleuth-meddler like you to know it, all gunpowder has a signature to it. A weapon used to blast out his brains would have left a lot of gunshot residue — residue that, if it was from another weapon, would have a different signature, but they only found one kind of gunshot residue on him."

"So, you're saying another person was present but they didn't shoot him? How can that be? It doesn't make any sense that Paul would go rushing through the woods at night firing a rifle as he went only to catch up to someone, argue with them, and then kill himself."

"So now in addition to your many other talents, you're an expert on how your neighbor behaved in his final minutes? Are you a psychic now, too? Have you figured out what he was thinking as he pulled the trigger?"

Regan remembered the scream she heard just before the final gunshot. "It's just that ... couldn't his killer have placed the gun in his hand after he killed our neighbor to make it look like he shot himself? Someone could have held Paul's gun against his head, fired, and put the gun in his hand before Tom found him."

"Sure, they could have. The argument you and Tom heard could have been the real killer and the vic arguing over the gun. 'I want it. No, I want it. Give it to me.' There were no signs of a struggle. I don't care how persuasive the other guy was, do you think your neighbor would turn over his weapon and say, 'Here you go. I'll open my mouth wide and hold still while you put my gun in it and pull the trigger'?"

Regan spoke hesitantly as she began to understand what Dave said. "Paul shot ..."

"Yeah Regan. No one held a gun to his head. He ate the bullet that killed him. Like I said, the investigation is in the early stages. There'll be an autopsy. Head wounds are messy so they have to look pretty close. I think they'll maybe run something like a light or a wire through what's left of the guy's head to track the bullet's path" — Dave was pleased to note that his made up description of how a head wound was autopsied caused her to wince slightly — "but they'll figure out the bullet's trajectory, look at the powder burns at the wound entry, and they'll be able to tell for sure if the weapon was being held by your neighbor or someone else when it was fired.

"If the coroner's preliminary findings hold up, he's gonna' rule a suicide and that's gonna' be the end of it, never mind what you heard or what your pal appeared to be doing at night in the woods. Be prepared for that, Regan. A simple suicide may be all there was to the end of your neighbor's life."

She stared steadily at Dave, neither nodding nor disagreeing with him outwardly, and sighed loudly. *Oh, I doubt that,* she told herself. *I doubt that very much.*

The news didn't change in the next couple of days and by Saturday reports confirmed that the coroner had ruled Paul Valentine's death a suicide. The announcement, no longer deemed juicy enough to warrant airtime on a news broadcast filled with more exciting local happenings like the student art print sale at UCSC or the Monterey Wine Festival, was given only a tiny half column in the *Santa Cruz Sentinel Local News* section. Regan might have missed the article if Tom hadn't pointed it out.

"Dave told me the coroner made a ruling on our neighbor's death. Here's the story," he said as he handed her the paper.

"That's it?" she complained. "I think I'll give Dave a call."

Tom stopped her before she could reach for the phone. "Dave and I already talked. He knew you wouldn't be satisfied with the ruling and asked me to break the news to you."

"Do you believe the coroner's right?"

Tom hesitated for some time before answering. "It doesn't

seem consistent with what we heard before Paul died. But you know how unreliable eye witnesses can be and we only heard what seemed to be happening, so we're even less reliable than someone who heard and saw. In the immortal words of Ben Franklin and the even more renowned Marvin Gaye, 'Believe none of what you hear.'" Tom shrugged.

"Besides, all the evidence — you know, the real stuff, the scientific, impartial, measurable data — points to the coroner's conclusion being the correct one."

"You didn't answer my question."

"You noticed."

"Well?"

Tom took a deep breath and blew it out through clenched teeth. He knew his answer would cause trouble. "I think what the coroner concluded is only the beginning of our dead neighbor's story. Paul may have pulled the trigger, but ending his life wasn't what he set out to do.

"My impression is that he was chasing someone, firing his rifle at him, and probably trying to harm him rather than just chase him off his property, or he would have stopped his pursuit long before he got to our back slope.

"He may have emptied his rifle, but we know his handgun still had bullets because he used one to shoot himself. How could the person he was pursuing have forced him to turn the gun on himself? He could have finished what he started with the bullets in his handgun."

"Dave mentioned another set of footprints were found near the body, so maybe the other person forced Paul to kill himself," Regan suggested.

"I don't understand how he could have been forced to take

his own life if he still had bullets in his handgun and, therefore, the means to fight to save himself. And if he somehow was forced to commit suicide, to my way of thinking, that makes his death murder."

Regan nodded slowly. "What are we going to do?"

"Logically I should be telling you there's nothing we can do except let it go."

"We heard the last moments of our neighbor's life, in a bizarre way shared them with him. Granted we didn't know him well, but that's such an intimate connection; I don't think I can let it go." Regan squirmed as she spoke.

"That's why I'm not suggesting what logic says I should. We can't pretend the coroner's report is the end of this for us. I don't know what good we can do, sweetheart, but we need to ask some questions and see what happens. We were both there when our neighbor died, so however we work on this, we're going to do it together."

Regan threw her arms around his neck and kissed him.

🏠🏠🏠🏠🏠🏠🏠🏠🏠🏠🏠

By morning they had, if not a plan, starting points. Tom would call the current listing broker and ask him a few questions; Regan's work would begin by talking with Gretchen at an open house she was holding on Sunday.

Gretchen Howell had clients who expected an open house every Sunday from 1:00 to 4:00 until their house sold. They had received offers, but the homeowners passed on all of them and Gretchen's commitment dragged on. No need to summon Gretchen to her office; Sunday's open house would give Regan the informal chat venue with the agent she needed.

She planned her arrival for fifteen minutes before the open house was due to end, knowing that the sellers' absence would be required until after closing time. On her way, Regan surreptitiously collected Gretchen's open house signs to ensure their privacy. Her actions ended all possibility the perfect buyer might find the house a minute before 4:00. Regan's conscience yelped as she put each sign in her trunk. She resolved to pay for Gretchen's open house ad to assuage her guilt.

When Regan reached the house, the front door, recessed by the deep deck landing at the top of stairs, was open wide. A large handwritten sign taped to the doorjamb asked attendees to remove their shoes in the foyer.

Regan dutifully complied. She wandered through the living room and dining room on silent stockinged feet before finding a pensive Gretchen stationed on a kitchen island stool with her back to the dining room.

Regan was about to say something in greeting when she saw Gretchen pull a Kleenex out of her jacket pocket, dab at her eyes, and then use the tissue to loudly blow her nose.

Regan tried to get close enough that she would be seen before she spoke, but her attempt failed. "Gretchen?"

The agent startled and spun to face her, almost losing her balance and her stool perch in the process.

"Regan! I didn't hear you come in." Gretchen's eyes were red rimmed; she took one more dab at them with the used tissue. "You startled me."

"Are you OK?" Regan asked.

Gretchen fluttered a hand dismissively. "Yes. Of course. Stupid allergies. I'm sorry; I know I look terrible," she snuffled. "It doesn't matter. The only people who came by were some neighbors who come every week to taunt me that the house hasn't sold."

"You're a very capable agent. You shouldn't let them make you so unhappy."

"Oh, they didn't. Like I said, it's allergies. Acacias, I think." Gretchen pocketed the now soggy tissue, forced a smile, and put a perky tone in her voice. "It must be 4:00 by now. Or at least close enough to be quitting time."

"I'm sure it is." Regan slid on to the kitchen stool next to her. "But before you go, could I take some of your free time to ask you a couple of questions?"

"Sure," Gretchen replied with too much enthusiasm as she stacked her flyers and guest book and began writing a short note for her clients. "What about?"

"About your listing with Paul Valentine."

Gretchen stopped writing. She blinked rapidly and Regan noticed her eyes glistened. She hastily wiped at them with her free hand and produced an unconvincing sneeze before returning to her client report. "Why do you want to know about that listing?" she asked evenly.

"It's all over the news and certainly has been a point of chatter in the office so I'm sure you've heard that Paul Valentine committed suicide. He was close to our house when he killed himself. Tom and I overheard … what happened. I hoped because you worked with him you might have some ideas about why he ended his life. Have you spoken to him recently?"

"No," Gretchen said emphatically. "Besides, he wouldn't tell me anything if I had." Gretchen sat upright, her entire body rigid, as if the slightest lapse in her posture would be her undoing.

"I looked at the listing file. Your listing was cancelled early. Why did he want out of it?"

Gretchen closed her eyes and took a deep breath. "He didn't. I cancelled it."

"After you invested so much money in advertising? I don't understand," Regan pressed.

"I didn't want to see him anymore." Gretchen's chin trembled as she spoke. "I couldn't take being around him."

Her eyes filled with tears again, but this time she didn't pretend they were caused by allergies. Tears cascaded freely down her cheeks and her shoulders slumped. Once she abandoned her pretext, her words came quickly as she told Regan her story.

"We connected at a meetup group for Santa Cruz singles. I was going through a horrible divorce at the time. He was, too. At least that's what he said. We hit it off. Oh, I know it was probably a rebound thing for me, but Paul made me feel desirable and sexy again, and after my ex left me for another woman, I needed that. I fell for him pretty hard.

"He acted as if he felt the same way about me. He said all he needed to finalize his divorce was to sell his house and then — well — he implied marriage would be in our future. He asked me to list his house and I jumped. I should have seen the warning signs," Gretchen stopped speaking and shook her head, "but I was so gaga in love I missed all the clues.

"He wanted me to list his house for much more than it was worth. I suggested he be more realistic, especially if we wanted to get on with our future. He countered with how he had so much faith in me that he knew I could sell it for what he wanted.

"Rather than disagree with him or show him the comparable sales and educate him like I would have with other clients, I behaved worse than the most deluded FISBO out there. I grinned from ear to ear and threw money at the listing hoping to reach some rich, uninformed buyer who would fall in love with the property and pay way too much for it."

"What happened?" Regan asked softly as she reached for the agent's hand and patted it.

"You probably already know better than to believe in fairytales, don't you?" Gretchen chuckled as she spoke, mocking herself with a bitter, sardonic laugh. "Nothing happened. Nothing except I racked up an advertising bill that practically put me out of my house and on the streets. And it gets worse.

"My sister is a server at Café Rio. She was working when Paul came in with a friend of his. She hadn't met him, but recognized him because I gushed over him so much that she knew his name and had looked him up on Facebook. Over lunch he yucked it up with his buddy about how his wife was never going to get her divorce finalized because he was never going to sell the house. He explained how the courts let the divorce settlement drag on as long as he had the house listed. He bragged about how he had this needy real estate agent busting her hump trying to sell his overpriced house and sleeping with him while she spent her money. He told his friend it didn't get much better than that.

"My sister dumped a pitcher of iced tea over his head. She would have been fired had she not been such a good employee and had Paul not told the manager he thought she tripped — she told him she was my sister before the manager got there to apologize so he knew he deserved what she did.

"Paul asked her not to mention what she overheard, but of course, she told me all about what happened. She said she wished she had been carrying hot coffee instead of iced tea. I wished she had been, too. I could have killed him when I found out how he was using me."

Gretchen leaned forward on her stool until her head touched Regan's chest and began sobbing. "So why am I such a basket case because he's dead? What's wrong with me? How could I still care about a man who treated me like Paul did?"

Regan put her arm around Gretchen and held her like she might have held a distraught child. She repeated, "There, there, there, there," in the same monotone she remembered her grandfather using when she was a tot who lost her favorite doll. It was a meaningless word, but one full of comfort when delivered with genuine sympathy and caring. It seemed to help; Gretchen's sobs became sniffles, and finally ceased.

🏠🏠🏠🏠🏠🏠🏠🏠🏠🏠🏠

Regan burst on the scene of Tom's Sunday dinner chicken grilling, ready to tell him all about Gretchen, but he started talking before she could take a deep breath and begin.

"I had my conversation with Paul's latest broker. It seems he and Paul had an ..." Tom enunciated his next word carefully for emphasis, "arrangement about the listing. He took it at an unrealistically high price, and in exchange for it not selling, Paul told him he didn't have to do any advertising other than put up a webpage and add the property to the company listings page.

"Simon Jomes is the broker's name. He's about to open an office on this side of the hill — caters to Silicon Valley's newly rich who want beach houses or country estates — and thought, with an overpriced listing he could have his name in public on his signage on a well-trafficked road for some time. Paul even suggested, as part of their listing agreement, he could have his name and contact information on the fallen chair where it was sure to be noticed."

Tom took a sip of the beer he had on the grill sideboard and for good measure sloshed some of it over the cooking chicken. He was greeted with a burst of steam intense enough to make him step back quickly.

"Jomes is complaining that now he may make a sale too soon for his liking and miss out on all his expected publicity. It seems with Paul out of the picture, the not yet ex-wife told him, since she and Paul wouldn't be splitting the proceeds, all she wants for the property is what her half would have been and ordered him to drop the price to a realistic level.

"Jomes is going to lower the price to $649,000 tomorrow morning. He says, at that price he has ready buyers and hopes he can represent both sides of the sale and double his compensation. He's not a happy man, though, since the property will sell quickly at that price and he'll have to take down his signs. He thinks it's going to work against him when potential sellers see what the property sold for, and he may be right about that.

"That's my news. How did you do with Gretchen?"

"I made her cry."

"How mean of you," Tom said dryly.

"She was more than half-way there before I said a word. My talking about Paul pushed her over the edge. It seems they had a relationship; well at least they did from her perspective. She's probably still a little in love with the guy — hard to understand why, considering how he treated her, but love can be like that — but from what she said, it sounds like he saw her more as a convenience than a girlfriend.

"We may not have missed much, not knowing our neighbor well. He doesn't sound like a nice man. And what you discovered ties in with what Gretchen told me. He was doing the friends-with-benefits thing with her while keeping his wife from moving on with her life by not letting the house sell."

Regan held out her hand toward Tom's beer. "Can I have a sip?" She took the tiniest swallow. "I'd sure like to have a little chat with Mrs. Valentine, maybe see how she feels about being a widow."

"What's stopping you?"

"I don't have a good excuse to do so; it would be awkward … unless …"

"Uh oh, I can see the wheels in your head turning."

"We could make an offer on her property; it does adjoin our land. Wouldn't you like to own enough land to call yourself a Bonny Doon Laird? You'd look pretty cute in a kilt."

"The last time I let you talk me into a real estate investment we didn't need and couldn't afford, we wound up owning a house with a mummified murder victim in it. I think I'll pass, although the title is tempting." He flashed a big grin at Regan and his blue eyes twinkled.

"We don't have to actually buy the property, just make an offer on it — such a low offer that she'll surely decline it; such a low offer she might even ask her agent to throw me out. But I could insist on presenting it and have my excuse for meeting the wife and asking some questions before she turns us down."

"I know you'll keep trying to convince me your plan is a good one, so I may as well save both of us time and tell you to give it a try," Tom joshed. "You think I'd really look good in a kilt?"

Regan set up a meeting with Mrs. Valentine at the almost-ex-turned-widow's now solely owned house for 11:00 on Tuesday. 11:00 was when Simon Jomes would be there to guide his client through the contract Regan presented and, she expected, advise the woman to counter the offer at a much higher number. That was assuming both he and Mrs. Valentine weren't so upset at how low her offer was that Regan wasn't unceremoniously booted out the door.

Regan counted on Mr. Jomes being prompt, but not early. He was a novice Santa Cruz Mountains driver who would be coming from his Cupertino office, up and over the mountain range on twisty Highway 17 into Santa Cruz, and then up the unfamiliar country road known as Empire Grade the dozen or so miles from town to the house she hoped not to acquire. If she called Mrs. Valentine after 10:00 requesting an earlier meeting, he wouldn't be able to get there before 11:00 because of the drive's challenges. She and the widow Valentine would have some alone time prior to the offer presentation — the whole point of the morning's exercise — in case they weren't on speaking terms after the offer was made.

Every time she thought about the offer in her briefcase, Regan could feel heat pink-up her cheeks. She was wasting an agent's time, making him undertake a long drive, probably bending the Realtor Code of Ethics to the breaking point, and that wasn't even counting what she was doing to Mrs. Valentine. To make a bad situation worse, she was going to begin the day with a lie.

At 10:00 Regan put her plan into action. She dialed Mrs. Valentine's phone number.

"Mrs. Valentine?"

"Na' quite, although yeu haven't got the wrong pearson," an upbeat voice answered. "You should have asked for Mrs. Valentino. FYI, I'm Melody Buchanan tae all who know me and will be officially again as soon as I record my name change. What are yeu sellin'? I assume yeu are trying tae sell somethin' since yeu clearly aren't someone who knows the name I use, and dinna even get my official name right. Readin' off a long telemarketer phone list, are ye?"

Melody's words were harsh, but they were delivered in a tone that matched her name: in a melodious voice filled with a Scottish lilt.

"No, Mrs. Val ... Mrs. Buchanan. I'm not selling anything. I'm the real estate agent making an offer on your property today. We have an appointment at 11:00. I was wondering if we might meet at the house early. I haven't seen the property for a while and ..."

"Yes, of course. I'm sorry I was so brusque. Telemarketers drive me crazy; donna' they irritate yeu, teu?" Melody didn't wait for an answer. "I haven't been tae the property in some time, either, seu we can have a look together. I can be there by 10:30. Will that be soon enough for yeu?"

"Perfect. I'll see you then." She would have to sound nice, Regan thought as her guilt level soared.

🏠🏠🏠🏠🏠🏠🏠🏠🏠🏠🏠

Regan had parked at the property by 10:15, ready to begin playing snoop before Melody Buchanan arrived. She wasn't looking for anything in particular, just getting a feel for the property so she could concentrate fully on talking to the new widow. The land wasn't special: it had neither rolling usable meadows nor ocean views, but as promised, it could indeed lend itself to horseback riding if trails were developed along its ridge tops. And even from where she stood near the property entrance, it was clear that timber was concentrated near Empire Grade Road and along the ridges which were broad enough for easy access by a logging truck. Harvesting timber here would be easier than on many parcels and not require expensive methods like helicopter logging.

"I can tell by the way you're eyeing these magnificent trees that you have evil intent for them in your heart."

Regan startled at the puerile accusatory voice so close behind her. She spun to face Taylor Bingham, Bonny Doon's preeminent anti-timber harvest activist, standing with legs spread and feet firmly planted, not three feet from her.

Taylor was a compact woman, solid in stature; her penchant for hiking hilly terrain kept her fit and her weight from crossing the line to stoutness. She sported a robust walking stick that was slightly longer than she was tall and patterned with leaf carvings over its entire length, sturdy hiking boots with thick socks turned down over their tops, and well-worn clothing in the browns, greens, and tans of the land and trees. Except for the sour expression on her face and her snappish greeting, Taylor Bingham could have passed for a jolly woodland elf out for her morning stroll.

"They are infinitely more valuable providing homes for wildlife and storing carbon than they would be felled and cut into board feet, although I doubt you'd agree."

"Actually, I would agree, Taylor. I don't think you recognize me, but we've met. I'm Regan McHenry. My husband and I live on the adjacent parcel. Except for a few trees we trim each year to maintain our view, we leave our land natural and treasure our forest."

"I know who you are. You haven't cut trees yet, but your property is zoned for a timber harvest. You and your husband are real estate agents and everyone knows that means you'll be trying to do so as soon as you think there's enough profit in it. You'll ultimately behave no better than that money-grubbing Valentine. He was planning to decimate the landscape, you know. I warned him he'd have me to deal with if he went forward with his timber harvest plans. You will, too, if you try to desecrate these glorious redwoods."

Regan ignored Taylor's insult, smiled, and replied evenly, "Then I have nothing to fear from you. We intend to let our trees grow as long as we own them."

Her attempt at developing rapport with the woman didn't work. Taylor's expression turned even more sour.

"Own your trees," she shook her head and wagged the top

of her staff. "That attitude is your problem. You think you own the trees on your land. You are fortunate enough to be their steward for a time, but you don't own them."

"Well, then, let's say for as long as we pay property taxes on them," Regan sparred. She didn't usually try to provoke neighbors, but then she usually wasn't upbraided on sight like she had been by Taylor Bingham for imagined future behavior.

"Taylor, just out of curiosity, what are you doing on property that doesn't belong to you in any sense of the word?"

"I'm delivering a welcoming note to the new solitary landowner," she spit out the words with as much scorn as she could muster, "advising her to cease any thought of advertising or conducting a timber harvest on this property unless she wants trouble. That's what I'm doing here. I might ask you the same question."

"I have an invitation to be here. I have an appointment with the owner to discuss the future of the parcel. Taylor, I wouldn't want to keep you from your walk. Would you like me to deliver your note for you so you can be on your way?"

A black Tesla slipped silently toward the women and stopped, its quiet approach overlooked by both Regan and Taylor as they bickered. It wasn't until the woman driver slammed the car door after she climbed out that the two squabbling women realized they weren't alone.

"May I help yeu?" the new arrival asked, her "you" drawn out in the "yeu" of the Scottish Highlands. Her tone was full of authority and her question was designed to make it clear that she was neither in a helpful mood nor pleased to find interlopers on her land.

"Mrs. Buchanan, I'm Regan McHenry, your neighbor, here for our appointment."

Taylor marched toward the driver, jamming her walking stick into the dirt with each step. She held out her hand and the note she had prepared. "Read this at your leisure, but be aware I represent many others who will not abide the wanton cutting of trees in Bonny Doon."

She thrust the note at the new arrival and, once it had been accepted, silently strutted past the woman toward Empire Grade Road.

Mrs. Buchanan watched her until Taylor Bingham disappeared into the trees along the road.

"Interestin' woman," she said as she once again faced Regan, "I think na' a pleasant one, though."

"Some people think she's a hero and others think she's overbearing."

"What do yeu think of her?"

"Let's say she's an acquired taste that I haven't yet learned to appreciate."

"Oh, we'll get on then, won't we?" she said with her light Scottish lilt. "I'm Melody, by the way, na' Mrs. Buchanan." Her face sprouted a genial smile. "Have you had a chance tae look around, Regan, or was that wee dreadful woman barrin' your way with her big stick?" she giggled.

"I havena' been here since the house was built over the garage and before the roadside artwork went up — I hope you don't mind retracin' your steps if you have done — because I'd like to get reacquainted with my property now that I'm in charge of it."

"I only got here a few minutes before you did so, Taylor or not, I haven't had much time to take a look."

"Deu yeu ride? We could ..." Melody rolled her eyes as soon as she spoke, "I donna' know what I'm sayin'. It doesn't matter if you deu; I had the horses boarded as soon as I heard about what happened tae Paul. Poor things couldna' be left on their own and I donna' have time to come by every day tae tend tae them. I hope they deu well in their new home."

Regan thought Melody's eyes moistened at the mention of Paul, and Regan was filled with empathy. She remembered how raw her emotions were after she and her first husband split. Feelings, both positive and negative, didn't vanish as soon as a marriage ends. "I'm sure they will. You'll all be fine," she added by way of encouragement.

"Well then, let's go see the barn masqueradin' as a table, shall we?"

Melody looped her arm through Regan's in a friendly and intimate gesture and hauled her in the direction of the oversized table and chairs. Melody moved quickly, taking long strides, and Regan, slightly taller than her escort, easily matched her pace.

"Did yeu know a man from the planning department lost his job over these?" Melody asked as the double-duty artwork came into view.

Regan turned her head toward her walking companion encouraging her to go on. "There were rumors. Do you know what really happened?"

"Indeed I deu. Paul said the man was a pompous jerk who wasna' about to let him get away with buildin' a barn and pretendin' it was sculpture." Melody's giggle erupted again.

"He came up here and demanded Paul take it deown.

"Now Paul wasn't one tae say, 'yes sir' and he was quite the master of a goad. He led the planner into a quarrel. The County man threw a punch and Paul let him land it. And then he marched right deownteown and straight into the department director's office and demanded the man be fired or he was goin' tae file assault charges and sue the County for good measure.

"Well, Paul was of average build and I gather the County man was of big stature and younger by a couple of decades, too, and Paul hammed up his injuries. The man from plannin' was a new hire and he just as soon became a new fire. He went so far as tae send a threatening letter to Paul sayin' if their paths crossed again, he'd finish the whippin' he started.

"Maybe he was such a hothead he deserved firin'. What dae yeu think of that?"

"The community was abuzz about problems with the County," Regan gossiped, "but I never heard anything other than speculation driven by whether or not the speculator liked what your husband did."

"Oh, no? I'm surprised. Paul was a bit of a braggart when he got his way. I would have thought he'd told everyone within shoutin' distance all about it. Ahh, well, maybe his voice dinna' carry all the way teu your house," Melody chuckled.

Regan could feel herself blanch; unfortunately, Paul's voice had carried to her house. She smothered her feelings and forced herself to stick to the conversation. "The latest story going around is that the County is litigating to get the structures disallowed because they are so clearly being used to house horses."

"That's right. Paul was fightin' them, though, countin' on that little problem makin' it complicated tae sell. I think it was his failsafe excuse in case he got an offer he couldna' refuse. He didn't really want tae sell, yeu know."

"I gathered as much, what with the price he was asking and his mostly using agents who weren't up on the facts about the property. How did you feel about his delaying tactics? You must have wanted the property sold so you could move forward with your life independently."

Melody shrugged. "Paul was pretty predictable. I knew he'd stall as long as he could; I think he dinna' want to, as yeu said, 'move forward independently.' By not sellin' I think he may have thought he could keep me tethered teu him, but he was mistaken. I moved on anyway a long time ago."

"Since you were both still on title for the property, didn't you have to share decisions and property taxes? Didn't that complicate life for you?"

"Not as much as yeu'd think. In exchange for me lettin' him control the sale, he had tae take over the mortgage and tax payments. Granted, he got to live in the house as part of the agreement, but I didna' mind since I had somewhere else teu be.

"Sure, our divorce was never finalized because of his shenanigans and he never gave up on us. Why, he even tried teu convince me that divorce was a sin; he said his spiritual adviser, the Practitioner, told him that when he took up his old religion. I didn't believe that for a minute."

Regan noted a momentary harshness in Melody's voice as she mentioned Paul's return to his religion.

"And when that dinna' work I think he still hoped that after a break from one another, he could convince me teu give our marriage another go. Poor man, poor deluded man. We shared too much loss and blame for that teu ever happen.

"In some ways still being married teu him has served me well. Besides, since I dinna' plan on marryin' again anytime soon, my marital status dinna' matter. All I wanted tae do was take back my name, and Paul's dawdlin' couldn't stop me from doing that. So I let him think he was still my husband, connected tae me in his own way. Married or not, it was all the same tae me."

Melody looked at Regan full on, a coy smile on her face. "I donna' know why people are so inclined teu share their stories with real estate agents, but have yeu noticed that we deu?"

Regan nodded. "I have."

"Well then, here's another for yeu. I'm expectin'. I didn't think I would be after all these years, but I am, just far enough along teu think it's real. I was about teu start pushing Paul for a divorce, perhaps lettin' him buy me out for whatever he offered because now I deu want teu get married."

Melody laughed heartily and held up her hand for Regan to see. "Look at my engagement ring. It's a rock, isn't it, so obviously I'm marryin' well and could afford teu do that; James and I would deu whatever it took for me tae get free.

"But suddenly I'm a widow who can marry at will and we intend teu deu so immediately. For modern people, my fiancé and I are old fashioned; it's important teu us teu be long married when our bairn arrives."

They continued talking while they walked back to the

house. Melody produced a key as they climbed the steps to the deck landing at the front door. She didn't need it, though, because the door was ajar. She pushed the door open and cautiously led the way inside.

"Ahh, what's happened here? This mess looks like more than my husband's poor housekeepin'."

What they saw was clearly more than a house in need of some order and a good cleaning. Every drawer in the living area and kitchen was upended; cushions were off the sofa and chairs and on the floor; books were dumped off their shelves. In the bedroom, the bed was in disarray with the mattress and box spring at sharp angles, suspended between the frame and the floor. Dresser, nightstand, and desk drawers were also emptied with haste. Even the bathroom had been rifled through, the toilet top left sitting on the floor.

"Paul liked teu keep a good bit of cash at home and he was the sort who would boast about it. Someone must have heard him talkin,' heard he was dead, and decided teu go lookin' for some easy money.

"Deu yeu think they're still around?" Melody cringed suddenly and wrapped her arms around herself as if she were cold.

"I'm sure they're not," Regan replied quickly, trying to reassure Melody, but her own observations made her feel less certain than her words sounded. *If someone was searching for money and found it, they would have stopped looking. Whoever did this ransacked everything; they didn't find what they were after.* Regan found herself reflexively looking over her shoulder more than once.

Melody moved on. "It will be a cute house once it's put

back together. It is wee, though, isn't it? It looked bigger from the outside because of the garage below."

Regan agreed. "Our office had it listed a couple of years ago. If memory serves, it's only about seven-hundred square feet, with just one bedroom and one bath. It was billed as a carriage house with promises that a new owner could build a larger house on the property and turn this into a guest cottage."

"Everyone must have laughed at the price Paul was askin' for such a tiny house. Dinna' yeu ..."

"Knock, knock."

A sandy haired man paused in the open doorway, conscious of interrupting their conversation and taken aback by the chaos he saw.

"Oh my! The house didn't look like this when I last showed it."

"Come in then," Melody beckoned. "Just mind where yeu step, I wouldn't want yeu turnin' an ankle."

He acknowledged Melody as Ms. Buchanan and leaned forward toward Regan with his right hand extended while he used his left to hold the shoulder bag that was slung across his body in place.

"Simon Jomes at your service. You must be Mrs. McHenry."

"Yes, I'm Regan."

"Good. Excellent." He slipped the bag over his head and immediately smoothed his still perfectly coiffed hair. "Shall we get right to business? Ms. Buchanan, lowering the asking price on your property was an excellent move. I have a bag full of offers for you to consider; I can almost smell a bidding war. So, let's hear what Mrs. McHenry has to say and then we can have a look at your other offers."

He grinned widely, revealing teeth that were so even and so white Regan wondered if they were original or capped. He up-righted an overturned chair and moved it to a table where there were two other chairs. "We can use this table as home base."

Regan sat down, relieved to hear that hers wouldn't be the only offer being presented and reassured that she hadn't caused a fellow agent to be inconvenienced.

Any hint that she was taking advantage of a widow's desire for a quick sale was removed from the morning, and most importantly, Melody wouldn't be insulted by the stinginess of her offer for long. She could leave before Melody heard the competing offers and fully realized how bad hers was, and she wouldn't have to skulk away under the withering eyes of anyone but Simon Jomes.

Regan gave copies of her offer to Melody and to agent Jomes while she spoke. "You can review the paperwork, but the high points are this is a cash offer of $425,000 with no contingencies and a twenty-day close of escrow."

Simon Jomes ears grew pink on top, but his voice remained friendly, if startled. "$425,000? So little? How did you arrive at that number, Regan?"

"The house is small, and the house and garage could easily be built for less than $175,000. The additional money is for the well, septic, and for the land, which has limited usable acreage."

"What about the timber harvest potential?" Simon Jomes asked.

"The ability to harvest timber on the property is likely a fairytale. Before a harvest could happen, there'd have to be a forestry report done and permits pulled. There would be public hearings and considerable resistance by various well-organized groups. It's possible a harvest might not be allowed, so even though the zoning is a go, Santa Cruz reality may mean it's not. I couldn't make a higher offer based on an expected harvest.

"The same is true of using the property as a horse ranch. It's not realistic to count on that use being allowed, either, and as Mrs. Buchanan just reminded me," Regan acknowledged Melody with a nod, "there appears to be a related issue with the County that might have to be resolved.

"My husband and I would be willing to take on the County, and our all-cash offer means there would be no lender requiring clear title before the close of escrow."

On the face of it, Regan's price justification sounded reasonable, but Simon Jomes knew better. He rested her paperwork on the table, folded it in half, and then slid his index finger across the papers to crease them. If he had run his finger across his neck, the connotation would have been the same.

"Thank you for your time, Regan," he said tersely, his voice devoid of any of its former warmth. "If you'll excuse us please, Ms. Buchanan and I have several other offers to consider. Excellent all-cash offers, too, with excellent terms, I might add."

"What would yeu deu with the property if I sold it teu yeu?" Melody asked, ignoring her agent.

"No need to ask, Ms. Buchanan. I assure you, you'll be

most interested in these other offers." His ears flared pink again as he spoke.

"Considering your property is adjacent to and slightly lower on the hill than ours, we'd probably rent out the house and leave the land as it is to preserve our view and privacy," Regan replied.

She rose and started to the door. "Since you and Mr. Jomes have many other offers to consider, I'll let myself out."

Melody tossed a final query at Regan, stopping her halfway through the front door. "Would yeu be willin' teu change nothing for now and let me take over the property on April 17th? I'd like teu hold a memorial on that day. It would mean hikers and horseback riders would be everywhere all day long. They might spill on teu your land."

"April 17th?"

"That day is an important anniversary teu me; it was teu Paul as well. I want there teu be a huge observance of it. There might be a couple of hundred people — perhaps more — on the land if I put out the word properly. Yeu wouldna' mind, would you?"

Regan paused thoughtfully for a moment. "No, we wouldn't mind."

"I have your word on that, deu I?"

"Yes," Regan answered without hesitation, "you have my word."

🏠 🏠 🏠 🏠 🏠 🏠 🏠 🏠 🏠 🏠 🏠

Regan slipped into Tom's office, closed his door, and sat

down on the sofa opposite his desk, kicking off her shoes as she did so she could curl her feet under her.

Tom watched her movements with smiling eyes. "I see you still have your head."

"I do. I may have a flesh wound just here, though." Regan slid her hand under the edge of her blouse, unbuttoned the second button, spread the blouse open, and slipped her hand down to her cleavage. She tilted her head back seductively.

"Umm. Perhaps I should take a closer look." Tom pressed the remote control to close the privacy blinds on his window to the hallway and rose from his desk, willingly allowing himself to be lured to her side.

"Tom? Have you seen Regan? I know she came in, but she's not in her office." Their receptionist's query from the intercom ruined what could have been an entertaining interlude in their workday.

Tom pressed his lips together and sighed softly. "That's because she's here with me, Amanda."

"Oh, good," Amanda sounded pleased. "Regan, Simon Jomes just sent over your signed offer — no counter — on the Valentine/Buchanan property. Signed offer, no counter, good job; your client will be so happy."

Tom's eyebrows almost reached his hairline. "What have you done, sweetheart? Have we just bought something?"

"It was such a low offer — Jomes was shocked by it — and there was competition. She couldn't have accepted it."

"And yet it sounds like she did. Did you give us any contingencies or are we obligated to buy?"

Regan dropped her head into her hands. "$425,000. Twenty days, all cash, no contingencies. All she asked for was a verbal promise that she could use the property on April 17th to celebrate an anniversary."

The sigh that followed was much louder than the one Tom emitted previously. "Seems like we got a bargain." He flirted with sarcasm instead of his wife. "Would you talk to her and find out why she sold to us and ask if she wants to change her mind? I'll talk to Jomes again and make sure she got good representation. If we're still in contract after those calls, I better start working on where we're going to come up with $425,000. Cash."

Regan would have run over any associate who veered into her path on her speed-walk to her office, such was her eagerness to call Melody.

Her opening line came from her heart, not her professional head. "Melody, our bid was a low ball; didn't your agent have better offers? If you want to reconsider, we will let you out of the contract."

Melody laughed charmingly, "Ack, Regan, I hope yeu donna' drive such a hard bargain for your clients. There were other offers. I liked yours the best. I liked yeu the best, too. I know what I'm doin.

"After the 17th yeu can deu what yeu will with the property, it doesn't matter teu me. If you sell it at a profit, well, let's say that may help make up for what Paul put yeu through deuin' what he did in your backyard."

"Melody, it's not my business, I know, but what's special about April 17th? Was that day your anniversary, or the anniversary of meeting Paul?"

"Regan, yeu're so quixotic. It'll be eleven years ago this July that I met Paul. We were both takin' a class studyin' to become United States citizens. We were married the followin' June. Our daughter was born in April of the next year and she died just shy of her birthday five years ago this April 17th. Her passin' is the anniversary I'll be commemoratin'; there's nothing romantic about that day. But I want everyone who comes to celebrate her coming into the world as much as her leaving it."

"Oh Melody, I'm so sorry."

"Me too," Melody whispered. "She was such a bonny little lass. I grieve for her still every day."

Tom stepped to the edge of the patio, aimed the bottle of champagne toward the Pacific Ocean, and skillfully pressed the cork. The popping sound it made was louder than Regan expected. To her ears it sounded not like the sound of celebration among friends, but like the final gunshot she heard that night less than a month earlier. She cringed.

"OK! Impoverished — true — but a Laird of Bonny Doon nevertheless."

Tom turned and splashed champagne into their guests' outstretched glasses and then poured a glass for Regan and one for himself. He held his glass aloft. "To my wife, the lovely woman who has brought us here with her uncanny ability to get impossible offers accepted." Tom's eyes twinkled merrily; he knew his wife understood his back-handed compliment.

"What's your title, Regan?" Dave asked. "Mrs. Laird? Your Ladyship? Lairdess?"

"Not Lairdess, surely," Dave's wife, Sandy giggled. "Lairdess sounds like someone with a too-large rear end."

"I think just Regan will do ..."

"Then I second the toast," Dave said as he rose quickly. "To Just Regan."

"You know, Regan may not have gotten us in too bad a place with her offer. She did get the property at a great price and I've been working with the County to clear up matters with them. They don't want to litigate over the table and chairs. We've promised there will be no more horses boarded and that the structure will come down by May. With that in writing, the County suspended their suit. They'll drop it altogether after demolition so the only unhappiness remaining there is with the guy they fired for the fight with Paul Valentine.

"The house is rentable; we'll do that for a while. Who knows, we may like being landed gentry and decide to keep it. And remember, we've got an LA actor and a when-he's-not-in-college-or-touring-rock-star for sons. If Ben or Alex ever want to live more conventionally or closer to home, maybe we'll start a family compound."

"Yeah, give it some time for the news to settle down before you try to do anything with the property. I'm not a realator — Dave deliberately mispronounced realtor, knowing how much it irritated Regan when he did that — but I know a few things. Don't you have to let a buyer know if there was a death at the house? You guys would know; do you have to let renters know about your neighbor's suicide like you do a buyer?" Dave asked.

Tom pondered out loud, "Well, technically the death occurred on our property. So even if we did, we don't."

"You said suicide again. Is that the final determination about Paul Valentine's death?" Regan asked.

"Regan, I told you that's what it was. Nothing's changed. Guy put a gun to his head, end of story. I know it eats at you that he was running through the woods shooting his rifle before he killed himself, but that's what happened. You'd rather have it be murder, but it wasn't."

"It's not that I want our neighbor to have been murdered. It's just that it seems more plausible that he was killed than that he took his own life. Tom and I have been talking to people ..."

"Of course you have," Dave said in the midst of one of the best eye rolls he ever produced.

Regan matched his eye roll and upped the ante with a squint. "Never mind that he was shooting his rifle at someone and that Tom and I heard him arguing with someone before his death, and never mind that you said there were footprints found near his body which prove he wasn't alone when he died.

"Like I was trying to say, Tom and I have been talking to people and it seems Paul Valentine wasn't the nicest man you'd ever want to meet. He upset more than one person. Maybe he aggravated one of them enough that they would have liked him dead."

"You got a list of suspects for me, Regan, Tom, people who wanted your guy dead?"

"Perhaps it doesn't rise to that level," Tom said, spreading his hands evenly toward Dave and his wife. "But Regan's right, a lot of people didn't like the man. I've spoken to the brokers who held his listing over the course of the past five years. Not one of them had anything good to say about him. It seems he manipulated agents, made promises to them he wouldn't keep, and refused to negotiate when they brought him offers."

"I never realized you realators killed clients you didn't like," Dave teased.

"We don't," Regan said, "but I spoke with one of our own agents who he treated so badly that she said she could have killed him. Of course, that was right before she said she still loved him."

Dave leaned back in his seat, took a big sip of champagne, and laughed out loud.

"Then there's the planner he got fired," Regan said, "who wrote him a threatening letter ..."

Dave interrupted, "Yeah, we talked to him. Seems he landed on his feet in San Diego with a new job that pays better than the one he lost here."

Regan tried again, "There's also his widow. He jerked her around for years and did everything he could to keep their divorce from being finalized. She's expecting a child and wants to marry the baby's father. Paul's antics meant she couldn't."

Sandy perked up. "Oh, that sounds juicy. She benefits financially from his death, too, doesn't she?"

"The widow Valentine couldn't have been that desperate for money. She practically gave the property to Regan and Tom," Dave offered. "And if she's preggers, it doesn't seem like being trapped in a marriage she wanted out of stopped her from enjoying herself."

Regan took offense. "That's a rude thing to say, Dave. But if this was murder, you'd have worse things to say. You'd be all over the widow, saying things like she and her fiancé wanted Paul out of the picture pronto so they could marry, which, by the way, is exactly what she told me they plan to do as soon as possible."

"Yeah, but it wasn't murder," Dave flashed a Cheshire cat grin at Regan, "so none of that matters."

Regan was taken by surprise when Amanda announced who was waiting in the lobby asking to see her. "Uh, sure, show her in, Amanda." She wondered if she should scribble a note saying, *if you don't hear from me in three minutes, come rescue me,* but decided that would be overly dramatic.

The Taylor Bingham who Amanda waved into Regan's office was not only smiling, she was carrying a gift: a pinecone wreath festooned with moss, twigs, feathers, and, considering the other materials used, a wildly inappropriate red satin bow.

"I've heard that you are taking down that hideous table and chairs and prohibiting horses on your property," Taylor began without even pausing to say hello first. "Congratulations on your good sense. This is for you."

"How nice. Thank you, Taylor." Regan tried to sound serene and sincerely appreciative, but between a warm greeting and a gift, an acknowledgement that she might own some land, and the fact that Taylor was so well informed about their intentions, she was too taken aback to manage it. Taylor didn't seem to notice.

"You'll want to rent the house, won't you? I have a perfect

tenant for you. He's a nephew, well not quite, but he feels like that to me. He attends UCSC so your cottage would be a perfect location for him. He doesn't do drugs and he is very quiet; as I said: the perfect tenant. He has a perfect respect for nature and the trees too. In fact, his field is organic farming."

Regan wondered if Taylor was trying to say "perfect" as often as she could to subliminally convince Regan that her proposed tenant was just that.

"Well, ah Taylor ..."

"You know the rental market in the area is very difficult, so whatever you think is a fair rental price will be perfect. He's ready to move in this weekend."

"The thing is, we don't plan to rent or even make any real plans until after April 17th. I promised Melody Buchanan that we wouldn't do anything until after she used the property that day for a memorial service for the daughter she and Paul lost."

Taylor pursed her lips. "She's planning a little memorial at the house?"

"From what she said, I think it's going to be considerably more involved than that. She's talking about hikes, picnics, bike riding, and a huge treasure hunt through the woods, all activities her daughter would enjoy if she were still alive. She said more than two hundred people are coming."

"Two hundred people! They'll be trampling all over the land, throwing away their trash and breaking down the runoff controls that keep mud out of the creek. They'll kill fish and ruin habitat! A small service at the house is acceptable, but you can't allow all those people into the woods!"

"Allowing her to use the property as she sees fit on the

17th was a condition of purchase. I'm afraid I have no say in what she does that day."

"And I thought I had misjudged you in the past." Taylor's words were delivered as a petulant insult. "It's your land now. What recourse would she have if you said no to her plans?"

"Whether or not Melody would have any recourse is a moot point. I gave her my word. To me that's what matters."

Taylor hurled the wreath to the ground and stomped on it. Pinecones and twigs splintered and feathers rose up in protest of their treatment.

"This will not be the last you've heard from me! You must be taught to respect the forest! Your word? What is the honor of your word compared to protecting the land?"

The incensed woman thrust out her chest defiantly as she turned to leave Regan's office. Tom barred her way, not with intent, but because he had come to Regan's doorway when he heard Taylor Bingham shouting. He pressed against the door jamb and held his hands aloft like a man under arrest to let her squeeze past him.

"Should I ask?"

"She's a bit mercurial," Regan replied as she picked up the surviving red bow and read the card attached to it. "She was bearing gifts for me, her new pal, and even supplying us with a perfect tenant for the little house until she found out about Melody's plans for the 17th. Now life is back to normal: I'm once again an evil destroyer of woodlands."

Taylor Bingham didn't take long to make good on her threat. Within three hours a small, but very noisy picket brigade had set up in front of Kiley and Associates Real Estate's front door demanding protection for the forest.

"She's a quick mobilizer," Regan quipped sourly with her co-workers who peered at the group through the glass doors. "If you have any clients coming to the office, you might give them a call and suggest you meet them elsewhere."

"Regan, look," one of the agents pointed through the double doors.

"Oh great. Here comes the local news van; Taylor's doing, no doubt. I wonder if she's that well connected or if it's just a slow news day."

"I just locked the back entrance," Tom said as he joined the agents. He quickly did the same with the front doors. "Let's keep everyone outside. The last thing we need is a protest in our lobby. I want to be present whenever any of you leave, OK?"

Tom had acted just in time. A young man with long green hair the color of a verdant springtime lawn who carried a sign that read, "*Why do you hate trees? What have they ever done to you?*" broke away from the group and tried to open the doors. When he realized they were locked, he pounded on one of them with his fist.

Regan feigned a lighthearted laugh. "Do you think he's the tenant Taylor was recommending?"

🏠🏠🏠🏠🏠🏠🏠🏠🏠🏠🏠🏠

It was past one and Regan and Tom were in bed, drowsy though still awake, facing one another and winding down after rehashing the Taylor Bingham-led protest, when Regan sensed they were not alone on their hill. She peered past her husband and saw first one light and then another moving just beyond the low edging of their patio wall.

Harry, cozy and sleeping in his cat bed in the back corner of their bedroom, was suddenly alert. He slipped from his bed, hunkered down into a stealthy crouch, and moved toward the floor-to-ceiling bedroom windows.

The top half of a dark figure appeared near one of the lights, clearly illuminated by the barely waning moon, froze for a few seconds, and then disappeared again. Harry droned softly, making a deep guttural sound that could never be confused with a purr.

Regan's voice became an urgent whisper. "There's someone outside. He has a flashlight; I saw his silhouette!"

Tom tried to calm her. "It's a month since the incident; anniversaries do strange things to us." He spoke reassuringly as he stroked her shoulder, "Your eyes are playing tricks on you. You remember the light from that night and see the top of a distant tree outlined in the moonlight. That's all it is, sweetheart."

She sat upright shaking her head. "No, I saw someone."

Harry lunged at the sliding door, yowling.

"Listen to Harry; he sees him, too!"

"He probably sees a deer, or maybe the foxes are back ..."

"No. Someone's there. Look! He's shining his light at us."

Tom was rolling over away from Regan when the fist-sized granite rock crashed through their sliding glass door sending it tinkling to the floor in dozens of pieces. It rocketed past his head and landed between their pillows; had he not decided to have a look for himself, he would have been clobbered by the rock.

Regan screamed. Tom swore. Harry hissed.

Two dark figures vaulted onto the patio, raced toward the corner of the house, and rounded it.

Regan gulped air, willing herself to be calm, and looked for a marker — a tree branch or the top of the oleander that grew beyond the patio wall — to help her gauge the vandals' size.

Tom bounded over the shattered glass on the carpet to the relative smoothness of the brick patio and gave a bare-footed chase. From her perspective, while she couldn't tell the sex of either hooligan, Regan was certain they were many inches shorter than her 6'3" husband.

Regan heard the unmistakable squeal of a vehicle burning rubber coming from the front of their house. The sound faded as it sped away up their driveway. Tom reappeared in short order.

"A car was waiting; they jumped in before I could stop them. It was light in color, older, but I couldn't make out the license number. Have you looked at the rock? Is there a note covering it?"

"I think that only happens in movies. There's no note, but the message is clear enough. The person who threw it was short, although I think still taller than Taylor Bingham."

"They moved too fast to be her. My guess is it was a young man with green in his hair and a friend of his."

"I vote we drop it," Tom said before biting into a piece of strawberry jam-laden breakfast toast.

"You want to let her get away with it?"

"We may be sure who's behind our broken slider, but we'll never be able to prove it. Taylor Bingham already got her name in the news with that protest at our office. That's enough letting her needle us for one news cycle, isn't it?

"Besides, she won't exactly get away with it. You know she'll want there to be a story in the news, even if she can't have her name associated with it. She's probably scouring the *Sentinel* right now. When she doesn't see a story in the paper, she'll watch the nightly news, just hoping. When that fails, she read tomorrow's *Sentinel,* expectant once again, and when she finds nothing, she'll be gnashing her teeth in disappointment.

"Imagining all that gives me a great deal of satisfaction. More coffee?"

Regan held out her cup. "It is a pleasant thought." The corners of her mouth turned up in a cheerful and devilish grin.

"And we're not afraid or needing protection because of what happened last night, are we?" Tom asked.

"No." Regan shook her head. "I'm furious that Taylor got one of her lackeys to attack our home, but I'm not frightened because she did. She waves her arms and yells and calls people names, but I think she's all bark and no bite. You're right. The best punishment for a news-seeking zealot like Taylor is to not give her any."

"So, we agree to do nothing, then?"

Regan held up her hand with her thumb and index figure not quite touching. "Tiny something. I want to call Dave and ask him how to make a discreet police report. I don't want there to be an official investigation or any kind of a fuss, but there needs to be a record of what happened just in case we're mistaken about Taylor."

"Dave, I've got a quick question for you," Regan began.

"Caught you and Tom on the news, or at least your office. I couldn't believe it was you at first because there wasn't a dead body anywhere." Dave had a smile on his face; she could hear it in his voice. "Here I always thought you were sort of a tree hugger who liked little furry things — you and Tom adopt cats — so I was surprised to hear you're really a ruthless animal-habitat-wrecking-tree-hater; at least I think that's what your little pal called you. You know the one I mean?"

"The green-haired protestor?"

"No, no, the little gal who looks like she's ready to whack someone with that big stick she carries. The green-haired guy called you land-grabbing-money-grubbing realators, or something like that. Oh well, what do they say? Any publicity is good publicity?"

She didn't hear him laughing, but Regan suspected that was only because he had put his hand over the phone mouthpiece. "If you're finished, I do have a question for you."

"Shoot. Just don't accidently massacre any little animals when you do." This time he didn't muffle his chuckling.

"Some people were on our property last night. They broke our bedroom sliding door with a rock."

"What? When was this?" Dave was suddenly a somber and professional police officer.

"Last night, around one in the morning. We couldn't sleep; the whole Taylor Bingham thing was keeping us awake. I saw lights on our hillside — then someone threw a big rock at us."

"You both OK?"

"We're fine."

"Did you get a look at the perpetrators?"

"Not a good one. It was dark and they were dressed in black. We couldn't say if they were men or women, but Tom gave chase and thinks from the way they moved that they were men — young men. They got into a waiting car. Tom tried, but he couldn't read the license plate."

"I'm lookin' on my computer … why don't I see a report?"

"Because we didn't file one. We're sure it was a couple of yesterday's protestors. We don't want to make a big deal out of it, but it seems like the police ought to know in case things escalate. My question for you is how do I file a very low-key police report?"

Dave was silent for a lot longer than Regan thought he should be. "You and Tom gonna' be in your office today? I'll come by."

"You don't need to …"

"2:00 is good for me."

By the time Dave's visit rolled around, Regan, and to a lesser degree Tom, imagined there was more to it than their friend being overly helpful. They met in Tom's office. Dave declined the coffee Amanda offered, unusual for him. He produced a notepad and pencil as soon as they all sat down and opened it as he crossed his leg, ankle on knee. His unsmiling mouth formed a straight and serious track across his face.

Dave's procedural formality made Regan uneasy. She licked her lips and wondered why she felt a tinge of guilt: they were the victims, and since she was none of the derogatory things Taylor and the green-haired man called her, she was innocent of anything that might justify rock throwing. She tried a grin. "You look like you're going to write us a ticket."

Dave launched into questioning instead of responding. "You said it was the middle of the night when you saw lights near your house?"

"That's correct. It was around 1:00 a.m." Tom matched Dave's reserve.

"The people you saw were on the hillside when you noticed their lights — flashlights you think? Were their lights aimed at the ground?"

Regan frowned, "Umm."

"It's not a trick question. Were they looking down at the hillside or shining their lights in the window at you?"

Regan answered with some hesitation. "The hillside at first, I guess. But then one of them raised his flashlight and looked at us. Right after that, he threw the rock."

Dave didn't press; he gave her time to think about her answer.

Regan closed her eyes to better recall what she had seen. "Both of the figures had their lights aimed down looking at the hillside. They were walking and using their flashlights like they would have been if they needed to see where they were going, and they were swinging their lights back and forth to take in the hillside. Yes, they were studying the ground.

"The one who shone his light in our window didn't raise his light until Harry, our cat who thinks he's a watchdog, started making a fuss." Regan nodded slowly. "Yes. I think he heard Harry and that's when he aimed his light in our window. Does it make a difference where his light was aimed before then?"

"*Why* does it make a difference where his light was aimed?" Tom asked when he rephrased her question.

Dave snapped his notebook closed. "Need to know only, and you and Regan don't need to know."

"I think we do, Dave. This is our home and we need to understand what's going on near it."

Regan looked back and forth between her husband and their long-time friend. The two men were unblinking, challenging one another for alpha male standing.

"Tom's right. First there were gun shots, then a dead man, now a rock thrown through our slider. You don't think it was vandals last night, do you? We have more than a need to know, Dave. We have a right to know."

Dave looked discomfited as the policeman in him told him to be quiet and the friend he was told him they were right. "I shouldn't be tellin' you anything — and I wouldn't except I know you two can keep your lips zipped. I can't say much, but no, I don't think last night was tree hugger vandals egged on by your little pal with the big stick. Let's just say stuff is going on and your neighbor seems like he was in the middle of it. The fact that things keep happening right outside your house is a stroke of unluckiness." Dave made a move with his hands not unlike an umpire signaling a runner was safe. "Nuff said."

"But you haven't told us anything," Regan complained.

"What do the authorities think last night's intruders were looking for?" Tom queried.

"I wish I could tell you."

"Don't be coy, Dave." Regan was more than a little annoyed at her friend.

"I'm not," he snapped back. "The thing is we don't know what we're looking for. There are all sorts of rumors flyin' around about your dead neighbor, so after his suicide, our guys took a good look at his house, his car, his gym locker, everything they think he touched, and didn't find anything of interest.

"Our local CSI unit went over the hillside by your neighbor's body with great care and all they found that didn't belong there was that fork you guys said had been missing since your Cinco de Mayo party last year."

"Were the 'guys' you mentioned the ones who ransacked Paul's house?" Regan asked.

"Ransacked? No, the pros I'm talking about are trained to put things back so carefully, most people wouldn't know their house had been searched."

"Then someone searched Paul's house after your associates did."

"What do you mean?" a puzzled Dave asked.

"When I met Melody Buchanan and Simon Jomes there to present our offer, the property was a complete mess. It looked like it had been hit by a tornado."

"I need to let some people know about that. Somebody's looking for what we are. And whatever it is, it hasn't been found. Otherwise those guys wouldn't have been lookin' for it at your place last night."

🏠🏠🏠🏠🏠🏠🏠🏠🏠🏠

Regan paced back and forth on the patio while she waited for the dinner vegetables and potatoes to finish oven roasting and the pork roast to crisp. She swirled the contents of her wine glass and took an occasional modest sip, staring intently down their back slope rather than concentrating on the excellent wine Tom had selected to complement dinner.

She didn't notice he had joined her until he put his arm around her and rested his hand on her shoulder. "What do you think they were after? Animal, mineral, or vegetable?"

Regan cupped her hand over his. "Mineral." Her answer was decisive. "If Paul left something animal on our hillside, it would have been carried off by scavengers. Vegetable might have been, too, although something like paper probably wouldn't be, but then paper should have been found by the CSI crew that searched the hillside. That must mean it's mineral."

"What are you thinking?"

"I don't know — I wish Dave was more forthcoming — but something, green, brown, or camouflage, and small, so it could hide on the hillside seems most likely. And I hope it's metal, not plastic."

"Why is that?'

"Because tomorrow I'm going to invest in a metal detector — I always thought it would be fun to have one those — and spend my Wednesday day-off sweeping the hillside."

Tom's laugh was merry, "Dave will be pleased that your amateur sleuthing has taken a benign turn."

🏠🏠🏠🏠🏠🏠🏠🏠🏠🏠🏠

By noon on Wednesday Regan, the new owner of a top-notch metal detector, was home pulling her hair into a ponytail after changing into the shorts and tee-shirt she deemed perfect attire for spending a warm spring day on the sunny slope. She'd been given a lesson in how to use the disk-on-a-stick by the man who was delighted to sell her his most expensive device. He told her many anecdotes about customers who made fabulous finds at the beach after busy holidays and assured her she would, too, especially since she purchased the super-finder model.

When her tutor took the price tag off the device and rang it up, he predicted a treasure find in the form of a solid gold bracelet in her immediate future. But as Regan climbed over the low brick wall at the edge of the slope, she wasn't looking for gold. She had a different idea of what constituted treasure;

she just wasn't yet sure what it was.

She began her search near where Paul Valentine's body had been found and within a minute was excited to hear her new toy squeal a metal find. She pinpointed the spot, took a hand rake out of the tool belt she normally used for gardening, dropped to her knees, and began moving dirt with the care of an archeologist unearthing a Jurassic find. Nothing appeared.

A troubled Regan reached for the metal detector and swung it in an arc over her site. It buzzed once again. Reassured, she abandoned care and switched to a hand shovel. She dug with speed. Two scoops later Regan unearthed an old rusting iron nail, the square kind that predated modern nails. It was a find, but not what she was after.

She spent the next half hour meticulously exploring the immediate area around where Paul died using ever-broadening overlapping sweeps. The metal detector remained silent. She moved her search down-slope: perhaps something had rolled away from him as he fell.

By three in the afternoon Regan had dirt-encrusted scuffed knees, torn fingernails, a sore back, and nothing to show from her increasingly frustrated and haphazard search but another nail, a copper penny, two nickels, and a veined quartz rock which — since her salesperson/tutor promised pyrite didn't register and set off her metal detector — might contain the gold he foretold was in her future, albeit not in the form or quantity found in a bracelet.

Her patience, something she never had an overabundance of, was gone and the siren call of a hot bath beckoned irresistibly.

Tom found her still in the bath when he came home. The bubbles she treated herself to had dissipated, but the lavender oil she added liberally still scented the water which had cooled so slowly she, like a reverse frog-in-a-pot-of-hot-water, had hardly noticed.

"I closed up the office and told everyone to come here for the office meeting tomorrow, and after that, to work from home for the rest of the week," he announced sourly. "The green-haired monster still has his group picketing our office and he's reduced our capable Amanda to tears. The one saving grace is that the media has such a short attention span, they've already lost interest in covering the protest."

"Should I try to reason with Taylor Bingham?"

"You mean grovel, because that's what you'd have to do."

"You're right, and short of breaking my word to Melody, nothing I say would appease Taylor anyway. Do you think I should ask Melody to downsize her event?"

"Do you want to?"

"No. As far as I'm concerned, if it will annoy Taylor, she can do whatever she wants, the bigger the better. But if it's a problem ..."

"Everyone at the office will be fine, even Amanda. Worst possible case is we'll have to put up with this nuisance for ten more days. After that, Melody's memorial will be past and Taylor's group will lose interest in us.

"I almost forgot: how did your prospecting go?"

"Not as planned. It seems I have no talent for finding mysterious objects. Who knew."

Regan expected her husband to chuckle at her confession,

instead he blurted out with affected nonchalance, "I hired a security guard."

"But you said you weren't worried about the protestors."

"The guard isn't for the office, he's for here, for our house."

Regan's expression took an uneasy turn. "Dave didn't seem to think we were in danger, did he? Didn't he just call what's been happening 'unluckiness'?"

"If Dave's right and our intruders weren't forest radicals, we surprised those guys the other night by being awake. They didn't have a chance to finish searching, which means they'll come back and try again."

Regan knit her brow.

Tom plastered a smile on his face and tried to be cavalier. "Now, I could stay awake all night with my trusty putter at the ready, but I'd rather not miss sleep and I'm sure you wouldn't want me to, so I thought a security guard on the nightshift would be a good idea. No big deal."

"You're scaring me," she said softly.

Tom squirmed visibly. He puffed out his cheeks and blew air through slack lips. "OK, I admit the security guard was Dave's idea, and it's a bigger deal than I said. The brush-off Dave gave us the other day was his attempt at not worrying you. He called me this morning with the names of a couple of police officers who moonlight. He'd already talked to them. Everything will be fine; we'll be well looked after.

"Dave thought there was no need to mention anything to you about a security guard, that the guard could be discrete, turn up after we were in for the night, and watch from somewhere we wouldn't notice him, but you know I'm not good at keeping things from you. That's not how our marriage works."

"I'm so glad I have you," Regan said tenderly, "and so annoyed that my best friend suggests you 'spare me' the truth. Did he at least tell you what's going on?"

Tom shook his head. "Not a word. He still says we don't need to know."

An agitated lavender-scented Regan rose from her bath and wrapped a towel around herself, tucking in a corner at the top to hold it in place. She planned to let Dave know how she felt about his transgression before she was even dry.

It took only a couple more brief after-work sweeps with her metal detector before Regan abandoned all hope of serendipitously finding whatever might be hiding on their hillside. She decided what she needed was direction — a real clue — and the best person to give it to her was Paul Valentine's wife. Besides, Regan was curious to know if Taylor Bingham and her unruly crew were hassling Melody like they were Tom and her.

After shouldering her way into their under-siege office, she punched Melody's number into her phone keypad and was greeted by a lilting, "Yes, hello."

"Melody, it's Regan. I've been looking for a little tea room that does proper high tea, but sadly Santa Cruz lacks one. I'd like to talk to you, but I'll have to treat you to plain tea."

"That's na' a problem, Regan, just please don't tell a good Scottish woman like myself that you want us teu drink herbal tea."

"You needn't worry about that. The best tea is probably downtown at Peet's, although privacy there isn't great and it lacks atmosphere. Even worse, the tea will come in glass or rough-glazed pottery."

"Ahh, you are a true Irishwoman, aren't yeu, teu notice such things! I've had lovely tea at your office. Your receptionist brews it well; she's mindful that the water must boil, that the tea must steep, and that it should be served in thin china cups. Couldna' I come there?"

"I wish you could, but things are tense at the moment and I don't want to subject you to running a gauntlet."

"A gauntlet, yeu say? How exciting," Melody laughed enthusiastically. "I'm quite fearless, yeu know, in my quest for proper refreshment. Will Amanda be on duty at say 2:00 this afternoon?"

"I'll make sure she is. Oh, Melody, you might want to park down the street, walk into the parking area by the store next to us, go behind their building, and use the back entrance to our office."

"And should I wear my boots and bring a sturdy riding crop teu defend myself?"

"That's not a bad idea."


Amanda was deployed at the back door at 2:00 ready to unlock it and admit Melody. Regan made it a point to be at the front door where she could be seen through the glass doors and booed. She was the distraction.

But Melody ignored Regan's advice about slipping into the office unnoticed. She parked her Tesla directly in front of the office and strode between the protestors, the curls of her red hair bouncing with each of her deliberately placed steps. She made eye contact with several of them, and when her eyes met those of their green-haired leader, he averted his as if he recognized Melody as his superior and wilted in her presence. He let her pass without confrontation or a single word of disapproval. Regan unlocked the front door to admit her warrior-queen, and Amanda, rushing back to the front of the office, clapped as Melody crossed the threshold.

"What's this about, then?" Melody asked as Regan locked the door behind her.

"I take it Taylor Bingham hasn't sent her henchmen to your doorstep, or you wouldn't have to ask. She's unhappy with your plans for the 17th and hopes her public shaming of me will make me reconsider letting you have your celebration."

A toothy smile began on Melody's mouth as soon as Regan mentioned Taylor's displeasure.

"It won't, though, will it?" Melody asked quickly.

"Not a chance."

A full-blown smile brightened Melody's face. "I'm sorry she's puttin' yeu through this. Is there's anything I can deu teu make it up teu yeu?"

"She'll stop soon. We're getting close to the 17th; she'll have no rationale after that. The protestors may run out of steam before then anyway. There are fewer of them every day and they aren't getting any news coverage lately."

"Oh my!" Melody giggled as she hugged Regan. "Yeu poor thing."

"Amanda, we'll be in my office when the tea's ready," Regan instructed before she turned to Melody. "You may be able to help me in another way. Let's get settled and talk."

Regan suggested the comfy club chairs in her office and the women settled in, chatting while they waited for Amanda and their tea. Melody explained her plans for renting a bank of porta-potties, catering, and parking for the many cars she expected even if guests carpooled as much as they promised.

"There're going to be a lot of horses and I imagine some people will stray off the parcel onto your land looking for clues in the treasure hunt, but they shouldn't come anywhere near your house, so I hope yeu and Tom won't think you need to be home for shooing duty and will join us."

"We'd love to. And we can always have our security guard stay all day to chase stragglers," Regan giggled.

Melody frowned. "Security guard?"

"That's why I wanted to talk to you. Taylor's group will disappear, but we have a bigger problem at our house. The police hinted that your husband may have had something of value with him when he died. We've had strangers on our hillside searching for the illusive something. They threw a rock through our window and fled when we discovered them. The police think they'll be back and that we could be in some danger until they find what they're looking for, or until we or the police do. We were told to hire a security guard, which we've done."

Regan noticed the color drain from Melody's face as she spoke.

"So many people have been scouring the hillside, but searching it is a big task, especially when we don't know what we're looking for. Do you have any idea what he might have had with him? Was he involved in something risky or with someone dangerous? Melody, any ideas or suspicions you have could be helpful."

Melody covered her mouth with her hand. Her eyes shifted back and forth like she was trying to take in all of Regan's office, but it was clear she wasn't seeing any of it; she was concentrating on something else.

"Melody?" Regan touched Melody's arm trying to draw her back from her thoughts. "Melody, what is it? What was Paul caught up in? You know, don't you? You can tell me."

"We had teu try something, dinna' we? Our insurance wasna' coverin' costs. We were losin' her and so desperate.

"Paul turned teu the closest thing he could find teu his old religion. Promises were made, but the price was dear. Paul said na' teu worry because he had been offered a way. Fault us for tryin, for hopin', but we did. What else could we deu?" Melody's voice broke as she pleaded for Regan's understanding. "Yeu take a path thinkin' you'll travel down it for just a bit, but then there's always more and yeu canna' turn back. Your sins hold yeu."

"Tea is served," a smiling Amanda announced as she produced a tray laden with two china teacups, a pretty teapot, creamer, sugar bowl, and a plate of decorated sweets. "Regan had me get some tiny cakes from Kelly's Bakery so you can have a mini high tea right here," she gushed as she put the tray on a nearby table.

Regan only took her eyes off Melody long enough to thank Amanda for her efforts, but by the time the receptionist left and Regan turned her attention back to her guest, Melody was transformed. She was the warrior queen again, head held high and eyes fierce.

"Melody, you were saying something important before Amanda came in," Regan tried to recapture the moment.

"No, I wasna'." Melody shook her head vigorously. "I was just getting' blubbery thinkin' about the past. I canna' say what Paul was involved in or what he might have had that's gone missin'. I am so sorry yeu and your husband are havin' to put up with all this fuss, but I canna' help, not in the way yeu want."

Tom was almost as enthusiastic as Dave would have been eyeing the array of little cakes and pastries Regan was arranging on a plate. "Is today a special occasion that I forgot?"

"You're not guilty of any oversight. These were supposed to put Melody Buchanan at ease so we could chat about what her husband might have been involved in and what he might have left on our hillside. You might say I was going to hypnotize her with high tea and see what memories would come to mind."

"Did it work?"

"There was hope before Amanda brought in my props. Her arrival put an end to whatever Melody was about to reveal. Before the grand collapse of our free associative conversation, Melody spoke of turning to Paul's religion and being promised help when their daughter was ill. From what she said, it sounded like there was a fee for deliverance, though — and not just the cost of prayer candles — and that

Paul figured out a way to pay.

"Melody mentioned sins. I'd like to know who Paul was involved with for spiritual support when his daughter was dying and if that involvement might have gotten him into something profitable but questionable.

"Do you remember Paul's brief FISBO timeout when he was having Sunday services at his place?"

"I do. We could hear music on Sunday mornings for a while there, couldn't we? If my memory is any good," Tom's grin was self-deprecating, "and it must be, since you assured me these little goodies don't represent a memory lapse, he only took a short break, maybe six to eight weeks."

"Is there a way we can find out when that was? More importantly, can we find out what his religious affiliation was?"

"I remember Paul broadcast invitations to Sunday services online. Let me grab my iPad and have a look while you fix dinner. It shouldn't be too hard to find out what you want to know."

Tom sat at the kitchen counter, sipped a glass of wine, and tapped his iPad screen for only a few minutes before he announced, "Got it. Here's what he had to say."

Regan leaned against him and read the screen over his shoulder.

"*Join us for a joyful service every Sunday morning in June and July. Practitioner Jarell Fitzwater will lead us in discussion and prayer from 9:00 until whenever. There is limited parking, but you are welcome to come on horseback. Hay, water, and comfortable shaded space are available for your horse.*"

Regan couldn't help smiling as she pictured Paul's huge dining table with munching horses standing under it while their riders attended outdoor church.

"Let's see who this Fitzwater is," Tom said as he Googled the name. When several pages of Jarell Fitzwater came up, he added Practitioner to narrow the search. The photo of a white-bearded figure with pudgy hands raised in a raptured pose popped up under 'images of Practitioner Jarell Fitzwater.'

"He has a nice smile," Regan observed. "It looks warm and he looks approachable, like Santa Claus during his summer break." She read as Tom scrolled the page slowly. "Reformed Church of Christ, Scientist. Is that like Christian Science?"

Tom was ahead of her reading about the group that Practitioner Fitzwater headed. "I don't think so. The names are similar but, no, here," he pointed to a paragraph, "Fitzwater says they began with First Church of Christ, Scientist precepts, but abandoned the Mother Church in search of a purer way."

"Does that sound like a scam or a cult?" Regan asked.

"Possibly. Whoa, they meet in Felton at 8:30 on Sundays at the Bigfoot Museum," Tom chuckled, "which, I'm sure, is in no way related to their beliefs."

Harry jumped up on Tom's lap and threw himself on to his back, front paws in the air, seeking not to cattishly play with the iPad, but doggishly to have his stomach scratched.

"This whole ordeal is starting to take a toll on Harry; he may be feeling unwell. Don't you think he's been acting strangely and looking a little peaked lately?

"I think I'll join the group this coming Sunday and see if

they can offer any help. Wanna come with me?"

"Could be interesting. Sure, I'm in. Should we bring Harry?"

At the second mention of his name, Harry began to purr.

"Let's see how the Practitioner does with us first and then see if he's willing to take on Harry another time."

🏠🏠🏠🏠🏠🏠🏠🏠🏠🏠🏠

Regan stacked another diamond ring — her grandmother's this time — on her right ring finger and held up her hand for inspection. *Glittery, but not enough.* She was going for ostentatious affluence and wanted to sparkle. She added a sapphire and diamond pinky ring for good measure.

Her engagement and wedding rings were modest — it wasn't her style to wear flashy jewelry — but just for the day she wished the diamond in her engagement ring was huge. She looked at her right hand again. *OK, it works.*

Her wedding rings might have suggested that she and Tom only had modest means when they married, but her right hand implied that they had done well and she had added luxurious pieces over time. The important thing was to convey that they had money now, money to spend for … she better get their story straight.

As she rehearsed what to say, she changed her mind and stripped off her diamonds. The closer their profile was to Melody and Paul's the better. She and Tom should have assets, but illiquid assets tied up in their property and business just like the Valentines. If Practitioner Fitzwater was a charlatan on the make or if there was a Lucifer lurking in Paul's congregation, perhaps the false prophet or the fallen angel might suggest the same path to them as he did to Paul.

Tom drove Regan's Prius instead of his BMW because it was less showy. "Do you want to go over the plan one more time?" Tom asked as he negotiated the twisty and narrow Felton Empire Grade from Bonny Doon to Felton.

"We've been over it enough that I think we know what to say and do. You just smile trustingly at the congregants and let me be the doubtful one."

"So, I'm basically just eye candy?" Tom teased, "Again."

Regan tilted her head and peeked at him flirtatiously. "If it works, own it," she giggled.

Their destination was located on Highway 9 past the main entrance to Henry Cowell Redwoods State Park on the outskirts of Felton. It was a smallish building, probably not more than fifteen feet wide and thirty-odd feet long and painted an unimpressive barn red, but it was impossible to overlook because a sign, which was a third as long as the building and half as high, sat on its roof announcing the Bigfoot Discovery Museum. The B, a capital letter fashioned with toes on top to resemble a gigantic footprint, rose even higher and caught the eye of all travelers due to an auspicious bend in the road that aimed traffic head-on at the building.

They found the last parking space near the museum and climbed the low steps up to the front door. The door swung open for them, manipulated by an observer inside peering through the door glass. The lookout was dressed in a rainbow-colored tie-dyed shirt, and from his look and demeanor, Regan expected him to utter "Namaste" instead of his simple "Welcome, friends."

The interior of the building was subdivided so entering visitors were pressed into a tight foyer lined with cases of hominid and mountain gorilla skull replicas. The space was so narrow that it was almost necessary to continue into the museum by moving sideways. The ceiling, which was covered in cheap acoustical tiles, was so low that Tom lowered his head as he entered, feeling the need to duck a bit. The ceiling probably lacked insulation, too, because even at 8:30 in the morning on a spring day, the building was oppressively stuffy.

The rainbowed sentinel led the way, with Regan and then Tom following. Once they rounded the end of the partition, the room broadened and the ceiling height increased, but it was still narrow. Rows of folding chairs occupied by people clothed in bright colors lined both walls partially obscuring more displays and a life-sized Chewbacca bust on one side, and plaster casts of oversized footprints ostensibly made by Bigfoot on the opposite wall.

Their guide hung back but motioned them forward. For a second Regan braced to run a painful gauntlet, but instead of blows, she and Tom were touched by friendly hands, patting them on the arm or cradling their hands.

As she moved between the rows of well-wishers, one woman on Regan's right jumped up and bear-hugged her. "We can't wait to hear your story, Mr. and Mrs. Abregetti. We are so glad to have helped."

"These visitors are not the Abregettis." The statement came from an unimposing figure — the benign Santa Claus from the internet — seated separately at the end of the room facing Regan and Tom. He was unremarkable in stature, but his voice was another matter entirely. The few simple words he spoke poured from him like liquid satin, sensual, wrapping them in his lush, smooth, and polished authority. "Join us, though, won't you?" He pointed out two empty seats at the end of the row to his left.

So powerful was his invitation that they would have felt compelled to join the group even if it wasn't what they wanted to do.

The real Abregettis, a couple in their mid-thirties, arrived as Regan and Tom sat down. Mr. and Mrs. Abregetti presented themselves like Regan originally thought she and Tom should have: as flamboyantly well off. The handbag Mrs. Abregetti carried was Chanel — it probably cost twenty thousand dollars — and her husband's casual loafers were Edward Green and pricey, as well. They moved down the parallel rows of congregants to greetings similar to those given to Tom and Regan, presenting each welcomer with an envelope.

By the time the couple reached the end of the rows, Practitioner Fitzwater had risen and taken a few steps toward them. He smiled broadly as he hugged Mr. Abregetti and then Mrs. Abregetti. Regan noted that since she and Tom had been mistaken for the new arrivals, the congregants didn't know the couple. Practitioner Fitzwater clearly did, however.

"Abigail, Adam, please, share with us what our Prayers accomplished on your behalf," Practitioner Fitzwater encouraged.

"Abby's shy, but I'm not, so I'll do the talking," Adam guffawed for the group. "I know we were promised that if you all were able to be together and pray with the dedication and concentration you were willing to give, we should expect miraculous outcomes, but your power has exceeded our hopes. My dad has made a recovery his doctors are calling unprecedented — you're doing, we're certain. Thank you all so much.

"There's more, though, and I give you credit for our other incredible blessing. We've been working on it for a while, but getting nowhere — in fact it looked like negotiations were falling apart — but we just finalized a buyout offer for my company. The turnaround was unexpected and the offer was, well, amazing. So, there's a special thank you in each of your envelopes, and Jarell," Adam took out another envelope and turned to Practitioner Fitzwater, "there's a bit more here," he chuckled, "than the amount we agreed it would take to cover everyone's expenses, but Abby and I insist you accept it." He turned back to the congregants, "All of you."

"What wondrous news," Practitioner Fitzwater intoned with arms raised like they had been on his internet photo. "Let's adjourn to the courtyard for refreshments and celebrate and enjoy one another's company."

Regan hadn't noticed him at first — Practitioner Fitzwater's presence held her attention initially — but once she did, he was hard to overlook. A stuffed Bigfoot: furry, huge, and enigmatic stood peering in a dark barred window behind the group's leader.

The courtyard was little more than a tarp-covered space behind the Bigfoot Museum and an outbuilding. Road noise from busy Highway 9 meant people's conversations needed to be loud. The sounds of twenty-some-odd people vying to have their voice heard added to the unpleasantness of the place. Regan put her lips to Tom's ear and cupped her hand for privacy. "You take the Abregettis, I'll talk to Fitzwater."

Regan excused her way through little groups of people until she reached her target. He was talking to the woman who had hugged Regan. Practitioner Fitzwater's voice, as loud as anyone else's, lost some of its magnificence with volume, but it was still mesmerizing. She listened without attempting to get his attention for so long that he finally shifted to include her in the conversation.

"We've not seen you before," he smiled warmly as he spoke and his eyes twinkled, "but we are so glad you've found us."

Regan expected him to ask her name and how or why she had come, but he did none of those things; he merely accepted that she was present. His lack of questioning flustered her. She fluttered her hands too much as she tried to gain control of the conversation.

"I'm Regan McHenry, my husband Tom is," she found him in the crowd and pointed him out, "over there. Coming here was his idea. He heard about you, about all of you, from our neighbor, Paul Valentine."

The hugger winced at the mention of Paul's name.

"Who may we help?" the Practitioner's question slid off his tongue with reassuring promise.

Regan, who she and Tom had decided would play bad cop to his all-in believer, impugned the Practitioner. "*Can* you help? Paul's daughter died."

"Your husband must know we can help or you wouldn't be here." Practitioner Fitzwater answered her challenge without ill will, but Regan had pushed one of the hugger's buttons. She was not ready to be so tolerant.

"Paul came to us too late and it took too long for us to cluster for his child," she stated defensively. "We did our best individually, but our prayers work so much better when we cluster."

"Praying together or not, I don't know how any of you can concentrate in this bizarre location."

The hugger shook her head, "Well, we did manage for the Abregettis, but it was difficult to cluster properly with all those creature mock-ups; I'm not the only one who finds them distracting. And we could only use the space after hours."

Practitioner Fitzwater smiled serenely, "We manage even here, but this is not our first choice of location."

Regan hesitated as if she were considering. "Perhaps we should offer ... no, I'm a non-believer. Sorry. Tom dragged me." She looked up and caught his eye. Right on cue, Tom headed toward them, smiling broadly.

"Sweetheart, I've been listening to the Abregettis. Do we need to discuss this privately or can I offer the congregation a chance to meet where they did before, since we own Paul's property now? I'd want them to start right away; time is of the essence, isn't it? It's the least we can do considering that we, of course, want to support the congregation, but after you tied up every spare nickel we have buying the Valentine property, we're strapped at the moment."

Regan mustered a harsh chuckle, "Thanks for consulting me before making an offer out loud." She acquiesced with a shrug. "Next Sunday, then? April 17th? You'll have to share space with Melody Valentine — you know her, don't you, Paul's widow? — because she has big plans for the day. She's having a special celebration of her daughter's life on that day."

Regan watched Practitioner Fitzwater closely to see if he reacted in any way to Melody's name. She could detect no signs that he did.

"Melody, of course." Practitioner Fitzwater said. "She's a lovely woman, and like you, a non-believer. We would welcome the chance to meet in a glorious natural setting and help celebrate Chloe's life."

Regan had never heard the name of Paul and Melody's child. Paul had never even mentioned having had a child, and Melody, even though she readily shared private information about herself, had never spoken her daughter's name. A level of knowledge, intimacy even, was suggested by Practitioner Fitzwater saying it. She didn't know what to make of that.

"We still pray for Chloe although we can no longer cluster on her behalf," the hugger added.

"I'll let Melody know the 17th just got bigger," Regan volunteered on the drive home as she and Tom compared impressions of Practitioner Fitzwater and his congregant Prayers, "although if Practitioner Fitzwater and his group come in the morning, they should be gone before Melody's group arrives."

"I vote we see how things unfold on the 17th without any forewarning. Let everything hit the fan, as it were."

"You can be a wicked man," Regan giggled. "I think I better give Melody a heads-up. Tell me what the Abregettis had to say. Was there money in those envelopes?"

"Most definitely. The congregants will gladly offer prayers asking for healing as individuals, but the Abregettis explained they do a much more effective job if they don't have to hold down day jobs and can pray together for a protracted time every day."

"That must be the clustering that was mentioned."

"That's the term the Abregettis used. They weren't charged a fee for services per se, but all the Cluster Prayers have to be housed, fed, and altogether taken care of for them to work together full-time for the best results, and there are twenty of them.

"Practitioner Fitzwater keeps track of expenses which apparently mount up quickly. The Abregettis said they offered half-a-million dollars for six weeks of the group's efforts even though they were told half that amount would suffice. They felt it was money well spent because his father's cancer went into remission. Then as a bonus, Abregetti junior sold his software company for so much money that half a mill seems like small change."

"A beginning price of a quarter million isn't small change, especially not to a couple struggling with big medical bills, and the Valentine's daughter didn't go into remission. Melody and Paul may have paid for prayers for a longer time.

"Did the Abregettis say anything about Practitioner Fitzwater making suggestions about how they could fund the Prayers? If he gave them advice, he may have suggested the same sort of fund-raising to the Valentines."

Tom shook his head. "It seems the Practitioner didn't. One of the others in the group did, though, or at least mentioned they should talk to him if they needed to raise money quickly. I don't think he meant they should use crowd funding, either, but the Abregettis told him they had enough money to go forward, so things never went further."

"Did they say who made the offer?"

"No. They just said 'he' offered to help."

"I'm going to call Melody. I need to let her know she'll have to work around the Practitioner and his minions on the 17th if she plans to do any early morning setup. I can ask her if she and Paul were approached by anyone in the group with offers of fundraising help."

Tuesday morning's arrival at work brought a surprise: Taylor's Tree Huggers, The Forest Fanatics, The Woodland Witches, Those Property-rights Protestors — all names that Kiley and Associates real estate agents had come up with, and several others too crude to mention above a whisper, to characterize the annoying swarm outside their workplace — had disappeared.

After inviting Practitioner Fitzwater and his Prayers to use the former Valentine property on the 17th, Regan had persistently tried to reach Melody to let her know what she'd done. She'd had no luck. By noon on Tuesday, Regan had left three additional messages and a text for Melody, but still hadn't heard back. She was beginning to wonder what had interrupted Melody's routine, wonder and even worry a bit, since Melody, who lived attached at the hip to her cell phone, was prompt at returning missed calls. She selected Melody's number for another try and was relieved to hear Melody's voice live on the other end.

"Regan, I was about to call yeu and ask a big favor." Melody spoke slowly and deliberately as if she had to put some effort into getting her words to form.

"Melody, are you all right?" Regan queried.

"Almost. I'm sore and banged up, but in one piece. More importantly, my baby is fine." Melody paused and took a deep breath before she spoke again; her voice quivered when she did, "They kept James overnight in the hospital. He's comin' home today — they say he should be fine, teu — but I donna' want to leave him for a minute."

"Oh my goodness, Melody, what happened?"

"I donna' know exactly. We had been out to dinner and were leavin' the parkin' lot. I canna' remember anythin' except spinnin' and then seein' blood on James's head ... we were in his wee sports car. The police said we were hit on the driver's side, so James took the worst of the impact. The driver didn't stop. There was a witness, but it was dark and she could only say what hit us was an old, dark SUV."

Melody's voice broke and for a moment Regan heard her sobbing. "Who would deu such a thing and then not stop?"

"Stay with James; take care of him. Promise you'll take good care of yourself, too, though. What do you need me to do for you? I'll take care of whatever needs to be done."

Melody sniffed. "Will yeu stand in for me on Sunday? Yeu and Tom. It's teu late teu let people know not teu come and I donna' have the strength or the will teu cancel. Everythin' is taken care of; all the arrangements are made. Yeu just need to make a little speech about Chloe. I'll write it; I have done. I'll get it teu yeu. Yeu just have teu thank everyone for comin' and tell them teu have a good time in her honor ... I wish I could be there."

"Tom and I would be honored to help your friends

remember Chloe." Regan was close to tearing up, "Don't worry about anything. The day will be just what you wanted it to be."

Tom feared a trick from Taylor's gang and it had taken until noon for Amanda to get his permission to unlock the front door. She had just returned to her desk when Taylor herself pushed the door open and made a beeline toward Regan's office, a satisfied expression on her face.

"Please, ma'am, please Ms. Forest ..." Amanda stuttered, dangerously close to using one of Taylor's infamous nicknames, "Ms. Bingham. Let me announce you."

"No need. Regan will be pleased to see me," Taylor said, waving off the receptionist as she hurried forward on her short legs. "We're on the same side again."

There had been enough commotion that Reagan heard it and recognized Taylor's voice. She was on her feet and prepared when Taylor rounded the corner of her doorway and charged into her office.

Regardless of what Taylor anticipated, Regan was having none of the elfin woman's expectation of pleasure at their reunion. Taylor didn't seem to notice Regan's less-than-warm welcome as she plopped down uninvited on a chair opposite Regan's desk.

"I hope you don't think me a cad — at least she's not seriously hurt, although I understand the man she was with was injured. But surely after what happened she won't have the wherewithal to hold her big affair this Sunday."

A smug tightening of her lips accompanied a slight wag of Taylor's head. "I wouldn't be honest if I said I wasn't relieved the Valentine woman's event is off. It is, isn't it, considering you didn't want her to damage the forest any more than I did?

"Now you have a perfect way out of the imprudent promise you made." Taylor spoke with quiet satisfaction. "Are you ready to talk tenants for the house again?"

Regan was flabbergasted but hardly speechless. "Your audacity is stunning," she said, fighting to keep her voice low and calm. "You've had your minions picketing our office for days, and even if the police don't think so, I think you directed some of them to break our bedroom window. Now you think I'll welcome you telling me who you want living on our property?

"I spoke with Melody a few minutes ago. After the little accident you arranged for her, you'll be surprised to learn nothing has changed except I'll be standing in for her on Sunday. Are you disappointed that after you had one of your flunkies smash an SUV into her and her fiancé's car, the 17th is still on? I bet you are!"

Taylor sat back in her chair and blinked with her mouth agape. She looked like an innocent child ready to squeak "not me" when asked who had swiped her figure across a newly frosted cake.

"Surely you don't think I had anything to do with Mrs. Valentine's accident, do you? I will chain myself to a tree in front of a bulldozer, picket and protest and work tirelessly to protect our woodlands, but I draw the line at causing injury to accomplish my goals!"

Regan delivered her gotcha question. "If you weren't involved, how did you know what happened to Melody and her fiancé?"

"I'm well connected," Taylor said, her voice dripping indignation. "Many people share my dedication and commitment, people in a variety of responsible positions. They give me information because they know I'll put it to good use."

Regan and Taylor sat in hostile silence, each clinging to their moral high ground and aggrieved by the other. Taylor didn't say more to defend herself and Regan didn't attack her with more questions. Their mute presence in the same room became a tense standoff, a game with an unwritten rule that whoever spoke or moved first would be admitting defeat.

Regan's insistently humming cell phone gave them an out. She picked it up, saw Dave's name on the screen, and answered curtly, "Yes Dave." Taylor hastily removed herself from the office, being sure to give Regan a final glare as she passed through the doorway.

"Ouch. You're obviously in a great mood. It's good I want to talk to Tom and not you. Any idea where he is?"

"After that greeting, if I knew where he was, I probably wouldn't tell you. All I know, though, is he's not in the office. Did you leave a message on his cell?"

"See, that's why I called you. He's off, as in off off: no greeting, no signal, no leaving a message, like he took the battery out of his phone."

"Wait a sec. Let me try." Regan called Tom from her office line. He didn't pick up, but his outgoing message was clear enough that Dave could hear it over her cell phone.

"Huh." Dave's comment was bare-bones. Regan thought of teasing him about his inability to use a phone properly and she would have, had Taylor not just been in her hot seat. Instead of a tease, she chose to make a complaint about Taylor.

"I know you said you didn't think our window vandal was sent by Taylor Bingham, but I think she was involved in our attack. More importantly I think she's also behind an attack on Melody Buchanan and her fiancé. Taylor was just here and she knew what happened to Melody; she wouldn't have known if she wasn't involved in causing …"

Dave overrode her words. "You mean about her hit and run accident? Naw, your little pit-bull tree-hugger didn't do that."

"How did you know about Melody's accident? And how do you know it wasn't Taylor's doing?"

"You like her, don't you, the Buchanan woman, not the little big-stick carrier? Let's just say she's on our radar and we know a lot about her. Maybe you shouldn't get too chummy with her, the Buchanan woman, I mean. Shouldn't do her any favors. Stuff like that."

"Since she's injured, I already agreed to stand in for her this Sunday at the celebration of her daughter's life."

Dave was silent for so long that Regan thought they might have been disconnected. "Dave? Dave, are you still there?"

"OK, I told you I had you on a 'need to know' leash. I thought Tom and I could keep your nosy little heart out of this, but you aren't cooperating. When you see him, tell him to bring you along and let's meet somewhere kinda neutral, like at West End for a beer and a burger after work. That place is so noisy no one can hear what we talk about. See you at 6:30."

Dave's phone line went dead before Regan could ask him again how he knew Taylor Bingham hadn't been involved in Melody's accident.

Regan checked Tom's office every few minutes all afternoon. He wasn't in until after 6:00. "We're supposed to meet Dave at West End in a few minutes. Oh, and I'm not one hundred percent certain, but I think I'm mad at you," she told him.

"How interesting," he smiled one of his best disarming grins.

"What have you and Dave been up to behind my back?"

His smile waned. He sat with his elbows on the arms of his chair and raised his left hand until he could contemplatively bite on the quick of his index finger. "Not much. We better get going; I'll tell you all about it over drinks."

It was still days before the NBA playoffs began, guaranteeing even more noise and raucous cheering at the West End, a former warehouse space converted to a trendy sports bar, but Santa Cruz recently began hosting a D-league team who had made it to their own playoffs. The local Warriors were in Texas playing the Austin Spurs and West End had picked up broadcast rights for the game.

It was good Dave got to their meeting place before Regan and Tom did, or they might have needed to share one of the bigger tables, but he had, and he had secured a high table in an awkward corner. The table might have held four, but Dave had given away the fourth bar stool, assuring they wouldn't have company. He stood and waved them over when they arrived.

Regan was wedged into the corner facing the commotion. "Why here, Dave? It would be so much more private at our office."

"He's afraid someone might be following me," Tom offered cheerily, "and grabbing a beer with a friend who happens to be a cop is different than meeting with him privately."

Regan didn't take Tom's statement as offhandedly as he intended, especially not when Dave added, "Exactly."

"Exactly who would be following you?" Regan asked her husband.

"Well, I did have a pretty interesting meeting with a fellow from Practitioner Fitzwater's group today. *He* might be."

"Is that why I couldn't reach you?" Dave asked.

Tom nodded. "Hector Gonzalez is a member of Practitioner Fitzwater's group. He asked if he could take me for a little drive to talk generally about what would be involved to assure a good outcome for Harry."

"Harry? Isn't that the name of your cat?" Dave queried.

"We've added Uncle to his name for the Practitioner's benefit, but yes. Initially Hector asked a few friendly questions. I played the successful real estate broker who believed in Fitzwater's work and needed his services ... but was cash strapped because of his wife. I think I must be a decent actor because he believed me and got serious pretty quickly."

"Sounds to me like you didn't have to do much acting after Regan's little land grab," Dave poked.

The West End crowd erupted at one of the Warrior's plays and Dave joined the enthusiastic outburst as if he were an intent game observer. As soon as the excitement subsided, he leaned toward the table center. "So, what did you guys talk about? Did he make you an offer?"

Regan quickly forgot her annoyance at being left in the dark by her husband and best friend. She leaned in, too. "Yes, what happened?" she asked eagerly.

"Hector is indeed the unnamed 'he' the Abregettis said talked to them about raising money for the Cluster Prayers. Regan, we met him on Sunday; he was the greeter dressed like a rainbow. Do you remember him?"

Regan thought for a minute and recalled a small man with closely cropped hair. "I do."

"He said he was a good friend of our neighbor Paul, well, Pablo to him. They grew up together in Colombia, shared the same non-traditional religion, and emigrated at about the same time, Paul legally and Hector less so a little later. He said, as young men they grew a little weed back home — maybe even a few poppies — so they knew the ins and outs of cultivation. He watched me pretty closely for my reaction to that news, but he went on, so I guess I played my reaction well.

"According to him, neither was involved in the drug business by the time they left Colombia, though, because heroin had replaced marijuana in the drug trade and the whole scene had gotten too intense and dangerous for them.

"Hector told me a long story about how Pablo helped him stay in this country initially and how he got involved with Practitioner Fitzwater, who ultimately got him a green card.

"From what he …" Tom joined Dave and the restaurant patrons in a cheer, "from what he said, he was a true believer in what Fitzwater's cluster praying group could do, so when he heard about the Valentine's daughter, he contacted Paul and Melody with an offer of help. He thought Paul was rich and could afford to spend whatever was necessary for good results. When he realized that wasn't the case, he arranged a mutually beneficial plan with Paul. Hector said he could offer me a similar arrangement."

"I don't like that he trusted you so soon," Dave said. "Smacks of a setup to me."

"You need to have more confidence in me, Dave. Hector said he was an HSP, a highly sensitive person who was a bit of a psychic and could feel the emotions of the spirit — that's his official role with the cluster people — and could tell my concerns and needs were genuine the moment he met me on Sunday. He's not so sure about Regan, though," Tom's grin revealed his clear amusement with Hector's assessment of his wife.

"Now remember, I was playing my part well, Dave, but he still had me disable my phone, patted me down for a wire, and insisted that we move to a more secluded location before he went into any detail about the offer; so he didn't think I was that trustworthy," Tom laughed.

"He drove me up Route 1 to just past Wilder Ranch State Park and pulled into a brussels sprouts field before he told me more."

"What did he say?" Regan was fascinated by what she'd heard so far and had already forgiven her husband for colluding with Dave while keeping her in the dark.

Cheers erupted again, but the threesome was too engrossed to notice.

"Hector said he and Pablo decided to go back into the marijuana growing business to pay for cluster prayers for Paul and Melody's daughter. It was convenient and feasible because of the parcel Paul and Melody owned. Paul wasn't worried about being caught because much of their land was rugged and unlikely to be surveyed by anyone but the most determined hikers or horseback riders. Paul and Hector cleared land near the creek that bisects the property, built a high fence to keep out the deer, and started to grow."

"What did Melody think about their farming?" Regan asked. "I'd guess she was willing to do anything to try and save Chloe, right?"

Tom and Dave exchanged a reflexive look she wasn't supposed to notice, but she did.

"According to Hector, they didn't tell Melody what they were doing. In fact, Hector suggested I shouldn't tell you, either, so we wouldn't have the problems with you that they had with Melody when she found out."

"What happened when she found out?"

"According to Hector, things fell apart. She demanded they stop what they were doing and that Paul stay away from him. Paul promised to do what Melody asked as soon as they finished harvesting their current crop. Hector said Paul insisted he take half the proceeds and used the rest to pay for more cluster prayers. Hector was furious with Melody for putting a wedge between such lifelong friends and for destroying his future income stream, but there wasn't much he could do about it.

"The Valentines' daughter died a couple of months later and Paul dropped out of Fitzwater's group. Hector said he didn't keep in touch with Paul. He said he wanted to, but Paul told him his marriage was in trouble and he was committed to doing whatever it took to keep Melody happy, which meant no more growing and no more seeing his childhood friend."

Dave and Tom exchanged another look like the one Regan noticed earlier. This time she didn't let it go. "Dave, you said Tom and I were on a need-to-know basis. You obviously think Tom needs to know more than I do. What aren't you two telling me?"

Tom rolled a hand toward Dave. "You're up," he said.

"Ok, so I told you something was going on in your neck of the woods. There are grows everywhere in the Santa Cruz Mountains. As realtors, you guys know how many calls you get from people looking for south-facing, private parcels with water on them, being on the grid optional, so you know what I mean. We try to keep a lid on illegal grows, but it's Santa Cruz we're talking about, so it's not law enforcement's highest priority, especially if it's small scale and local folks are doing the growing.

"We've known for some time there's been a bigger than normal production happening in Bonny Doon. It was small and run by locals until a few years ago, but then the rumors started that some foreigners were in on it and that they weren't only growing, but also importing via panga boats, and not just marijuana.

"There was a big article about it in the *Sentinel* a couple of years back when a bust happened at Shark Tooth Beach just south of Davenport. What they didn't say in the story was that it wasn't Mexican cartels involved and it wasn't only marijuana. It was cocaine and heroin out of Colombia.

"The panga boats are cheap and disposable. Guys in Tijuana and Ensenada are picked up off the streets and promised a grand or two to drive a boat up the California coast. They pull in at remote beaches like Shark Tooth and the stuff gets offloaded to RVs or big trucks.

"We've been getting better at intercepts when we see big vehicles like that parked near a perfect beach. But as we've gotten better at intercepts, the smugglers have gotten more creative, too. Before the FBI — yeah, they're involved — caught up with the Shark Tooth guys, a lot of the product got offloaded to ordinary four-wheel-drive vehicles like lots of people own. Everyone figured the pattern at least in this area had changed again and the cargo was being picked up and taken out in small batches to a nearby safe area where it could be processed and packaged for distribution in the Midwest.

"Now we know your dead neighbor was up to his eyeballs in the whole smuggling thing. The question is who was in it with him. Actually, who is still in it? From what Tom had to say, it sounds like your rainbow–wearing HSP isn't, since he's looking for a new arrangement.

"Rumor is that the operation was being run by a man and a woman — probably your dead neighbor was the guy — at least until your neighbor offed himself. That leaves the woman working on her own. She's good; no one knows who she is. My money is on your new gal pal, Melody."

"Melody?" Regan shook her head vigorously. "No, not Melody. Why would you think she's involved? Tom, didn't Hector say she wanted Paul to stop? Once Chloe died, there'd be no incentive for her to let him continue growing, let alone expanding to smuggling. Besides, she and Paul weren't even a couple any more. Melody filed for divorce. She wanted Paul out of her life, not to be in an illegal business with him."

"Who says business partners have to sleep together?" Dave asked. "If the money's good, who says they even have to like one another?"

Tom cut in, "It doesn't seem like she tried very hard to get that divorce. Think about it logically, sweetheart. She let their marriage drag on for years." He shrugged, "Maybe in the back of her mind she thought, if one of them ever got caught, as long as they were married, the other couldn't be compelled to testify against them because they were still spouses."

"Good one," Dave bounced up and down in his seat, impressed with Tom's suggestion, "I never thought of that."

"Melody told you Paul had some misguided notion that he might win her back given time and some distance. That's what she said, but perhaps she didn't want their property sold any more than he did, so that's why she let Paul play his listing games. If they no longer owned the land, it would make using it for their drug operation harder."

"But Melody was willing to sell. As soon as pricing was up to her, she dropped the price so low, the property was bound to sell."

"You don't know that, Regan," Dave admonished. "If you hadn't come along, maybe she'd have proven as difficult to pin down as her hubby was."

"But she sold to us, and for less money than she might have gotten."

Dave smirked. "Didn't that seem kinda too easy? You may

be a good negotiator, Regan, but you're not that good."

"You told her we'd leave the land as it was," Tom said. "No development, no people exploring or making waves, no prying eyes. We were the perfect buyers."

"She could still run her operation on remote parts of the land, but she could distance herself from the site. And you two upstanding citizens would be the owners of the property and take the confiscation hit if law enforcement caught up with her venture. Win, win for her."

"You're forgetting an important fact. Melody had me agree she could have hundreds of people traipsing over every inch of the land this Sunday. Why would she do that if she had a secret operation she wanted to keep hidden?"

Dave's smile was patronizing. "She's more than a step ahead of you." As he considered what he was about to say, he reluctantly added, "maybe a step ahead of law enforcement, too. She's got to know that by now she's on our radar. What better way to look innocent than by arranging for a big event and then having circumstances beyond her control shut it down. Poor Melody.

"The driver who caused her accident hasn't been caught. If he is — I'm going out on a limb here, but a big fat sturdy one — and saying we'll find he has a connection to Melody. So she gets him to tap her and her guy, not hard enough to cause any serious injuries, but hard enough for her to close down her weekend plans."

"But she hasn't, Dave. Melody asked if Tom and I would stand in for her so the event can go forward as scheduled." Regan turned to Tom. "I haven't had a chance to tell you that she asked and I said we would. So nothing's shut down, nothing's changed. You've got to be wrong about her."

Regan followed Tom home separately since each came to work in their own car. She tried to remember everything Melody had said to her on every occasion, but especially when Melody questioned her about what they'd do with the property. She couldn't come up with anything Melody said that indicated she would have any interest in the property after the 17th.

Regan didn't wait for the garage door to close before she took up with Tom where they left off at West End. "I don't believe anything Dave suspects about Melody. You know I have good people instincts ..."

Tom cocked his head and spoke volumes without saying a word.

"Well, most of the time I do — at least with people who aren't murderers, and Dave didn't imply Melody killed anyone. I don't buy it, her as a drug lord mastermind. Did he tell you anything else about her that he didn't say tonight?"

"He didn't, but Hector did. According to him, I shouldn't tell you if we went into business because, in his words, 'women like shiny things'."

"What does that mean," Regan frowned.

It means that Hector thinks Melody has expensive taste and that she encouraged Paul to force him out so they wouldn't have to split the proceeds with him. Hector's bitter about Melody and so he generalizes about all women. He's afraid you might push me to do the same thing to him that Melody did, once he helps me get our business up and growing."

"I want to meet this Hector person. He seems like a man who knew our dead neighbor well and for a long time. He may be the key to understanding why Paul killed himself. Tell him you couldn't keep quiet about his proposal and that I'm interested in it. Invite him to dinner so we can have a private conversation."

"Do we introduce him to 'Uncle' Harry over dinner?"

"You bet. I want to see the look on his face and find out if his belief in Practitioner Fitzwater's group having a prayer pipeline to cures is genuine or if he thinks the Practitioner is just interested in getting paid. Let's make it clear the Practitioner must know that Uncle Harry is a cat and see if that changes anything."

"And the Melody issue?" Tom asked gently.

"Melody isn't dirty. I'm sure of it."

"You usually get it right in the end, but since your habit of thinking the likable-guilty are innocent has gotten you into trouble more than once." He put his arms around his wife and pulled her to him in a tight embrace. "I'm going to keep you extra close for a while."

Regan smiled up at him, "You'll get no complaints from me if you do."

Hector Gonzalez was due for dinner at 6:00 on Thursday. Regan was still going to play bad cop to Tom's good cop, appropriate especially since she knew Hector was woman-averse. She was going to come across as the perfect hostess, though, and had researched traditional Colombian meals. Potato-filled empanadas, tidy little fold-over pastries that took forever to prepare, were on her list for hors d'oeuvres. The rest of the meal was a traditional Colombian banadeja paisa, a platter laden with red beans cooked with pork, white rice, ground meat, eggs, chicharrón, plantain, chorizo sausages, corn pancakes called arepa, avocado, and lemon. The great commonality all the food except the rice, avocado, and lemon had was that it was fried. Authenticity set off the smoke alarm in the kitchen twice as Regan perspired over her creation.

Hector's arrival was precise; he knocked at their door at 6:00 sharp. Stripped of the rainbow-bright garments he wore the first time Regan met him, he was an unassuming man, shorter than her by a couple of inches with brown hair and smallish brown eyes. He wasn't a smiler, but he wasn't morose, either. No trace of his birth-country remained as he spoke. Like Paul, Hector had traded a Spanish accent for an accent that sounded like vanilla American. His slightly unusual sentence structure was the only giveaway that he wasn't born and bred in the Midwest.

The thought crossed her mind as she shook Hector's hand that, without his rainbow-colored clothing, his looks were ordinary enough that he would blend in so well he might become invisible. The rigidity of his hand in hers also suggested he had already decided he didn't trust her.

They ate in relative silence whenever Regan stopped being a bubbly hostess. Hector complimented her on the meal and he wouldn't have needed to be a Highly Sensitive Person to realize just how phony her over-reaction to his accolade was.

By the time Tom suggested they move to the living room to talk a little business, Regan was sure Hector was as leery of her as he was of Melody.

Tom had been subdued all evening, just as he had been at the Bigfoot Museum, letting Regan be the dominant personality. She upped the ante once they were settled.

"Tom tells me you have a business proposition for us — well he said it was for him, but he doesn't make any decisions without my input. He's filled me in on the basics, but I need more details if I'm … we're … going to give your plan serious consideration."

Tom leaned back far enough to make sure he was just out of Regan's peripheral view and mouthed "Sorry" to Hector.

"Don't worry, though. We're not snitches. If we decide we don't want to be part of your plan, we won't tell anyone what you proposed, not even Practitioner Fitzwater, who probably knows all about it already anyway."

Hector's protest was immediate and he seemed genuinely horrified at Regan's suggestion. "No, no, he doesn't. His work is so important; he's a great man, not like the rest of us. He would never allow any of his congregation to be involved in such dealings. You must promise me on your grandmother's grave that you would never tell Practitioner Fitzwater how much my heart has fallen."

"You have our word," Tom spoke quickly.

Hector stared intently at Regan.

"Mine, too," she said after a measured pause.

"Then we can talk freely. Pablo and I were country-raised and had practice as farmers of many kinds of crops. We cleared some space down by the creek that runs through his, well now, your property. The fence is probably still in place and the area perhaps weedy, but it shouldn't take much to return it to good condition. We were able to use creek water, but following California's drought, I don't know about the amount of water that may remain. We might need to dig a shallow well. After that, it's pretty easy to grow marijuana."

"I don't see myself as a farmer, gentleman or not," Tom said. "I spend my time at real estate work."

Hector pondered and then brightened. "Well, then we could use the house on the property. It has a big garage that would be easily converted to a grow room if we bought lights, and there's plenty of water connected from the property well."

"We've heard rumors about a man and woman already using the property for growing ... and importing ..." Regan let her statement trail off and watched Hector closely for his reaction.

"Yes. I've heard that, too," Hector spit out his words. "But we wouldn't be big time. If we keep our operation small, we should be fine. Besides, I think Pablo was the man, and that his wife took over my place after she forced me out, which means you only have her to deal with.

"You women stick together, don't you, better than men do? Perhaps if you let her know you know and don't care about what she's doing, she won't mind our having a small grow.

"It would be my preference to get rid of her, but since it seems she can't be done away with, who knows, if you, Mrs. McHenry, ask her nicely, maybe for a cut of our profits, she might even let us use her marketing connections."

Regan put on her best poker face at the mention of Melody and tried not to react, but she had never mastered keeping the pink out of her face. She was glad Hector put in his barb about females so, if he noticed her flaming cheeks, he could blame it on her annoyance at his statement.

Tom covered for her even more. "We do need the money, sweetheart, for Uncle Harry. I think we should formalize an agreement."

As if on cue at the sound of his name Harry bounded into the room and rubbed against Hector's leg.

"Uncle Harry," Tom reprimanded, "stop that. You're shedding on our guest."

Hector was so startled by Tom calling the cat Uncle Harry that he abandoned his perfectly accent-free English for his native tongue. "Su tío Harry es un gato?" he exclaimed.

"Yes," Regan responded.

115

"No," Tom corrected forcefully.

Regan offered her own explanation. "He's a trans-species cat: he's a dog in a cat's body, at least that's what Tom thinks Uncle Harry is."

"That's only part of it," Tom said. "My Uncle Harry and I were very close and Uncle Harry and his dog, Harry, were even closer. When he was on his deathbed, I promised my uncle I'd look after his pet. A few weeks after Uncle Harry died, his dog died. And a few weeks after that, Harry the cat turned up at our house, a wet and starving kitten. I think he's my dead Uncle Harry's dog reborn in a cat's body.

"My Uncle Harry is still watching over us; I can often feel his presence. He wants me to take good care of his pet and Uncle Harry the cat is not doing well. That's why we need Practitioner Fitzwater's Prayers to help him."

Regan asked guilelessly, "The Practitioner does believe in helping all beings, doesn't he, even the human-challenged?"

"He will help all in need; that is his mission." His face was pale and Hector sputtered, but his accent was once again suppressed. "He will try to help even a cat and even without pay because he is a good man. I have changed my mind about working with you, however, at least for a while.

"I like you," Hector directed his words at Tom, "and I wanted to help you raise money so the group can cluster for more powerful prayers, but given what you have told me about your real uncle's presence, I cannot work with you, not while these spirits walk.

"I may detest Pablo's wife, but I do not fear her. But this, this is too much," he shook his head solemnly, "because I do fear the spirits. As much as you need money for the

Practitioner's best help for your ..." he hesitated and held his hands in front of his chest protectively, "creature ... and I need money for myself ... after what you said, I know the land you own, this whole place, is filled with too many spirits of the dead. I have seen what they can do with my own eyes. Therefore, I cannot help you. If I do, I'm afraid they will come for me, too."

Hector jerked to his feet, arms akimbo, so quickly it looked like he was a marionette pulled up by someone holding his strings and controlling him from above.

"I am sorry. I wish you well and that you are safe from the dead. Good luck." He glared at Regan, "For raising money right now, try talking to Pablo's wife. I will show myself out."

He got to the door, put his hand on the door handle and then didn't move. "It's dark outside. Could I ask you, please, to put on the lights until I am gone?"

Tom complied. He left the lights on until the taillights of Hector's car disappeared around the bend in the driveway.

"Wow." Tom clamped his mouth shut.

"Uh huh. I guess we overdid it about Harry."

"That's not what I meant." He gave Regan a few seconds to reach the same conclusion he had. When she said nothing, he added, "It sounds like Dave is right about Melody."

"It does sound like Hector thinks so, but he has so much animosity toward her, he probably can't think straight about her. What's interesting to me is his comment about spirits of the dead. What did you make of that?"

"Not much. I'm hardly an expert on what the rural Colombian belief system is, but my guess is it contains some supernatural holdovers from pre-European times mixed in with the predominant Catholic faith. If Hector grew up in the countryside, he may still be influenced by some of those childhood beliefs. Certainly his involvement with Practitioner Fitzwater indicates he's open to less than mainstream religious groups and thoughts and he may believe in malevolent spirits and ghosts.

"Fortunately, I don't, so I'm not worried about our land being haunted. My only concern is for the very real and living who may be trespassing. They're the ones who could be dangerous … which brings me back to Melody. As much as you don't want to believe it, she has two strikes against her from two different directions."

"You're right." Regan was pensive. "I don't want to believe she's a female drug lord, and all my instincts about her say she isn't. But if I'm mistaken and Dave and Hector aren't, and she has some agenda that I don't understand, we need to know about it because we sure don't want to help her.

"If she's up to something it's probably scheduled for the 17th. Tom, do you think her accident was staged so she could put us in charge of the day?"

"Dave surely had suspicions that she knew her attacker. An SUV versus a sports car and only minimal injuries? It's not much of a stretch to say she had to be part of arranging the accident."

"Her fiancé was hurt, though. He spent the night in the hospital. Would she risk endangering him? Couldn't she have arranged an accident when only she was in the car?"

"She could have, of course, but then logically she would have had to turn the 17th over to him, not us. You know how emergency rooms are; his spending the night in the hospital may not have been that big a deal. They could have kept him overnight for observation, especially if he complained of being disoriented and had a head wound. As far as that goes, if he was in on it, he and Melody could have cut his head and he could have faked the rest.

"Like Dave, Hector said a man and a woman were in charge. Melody might have pushed Hector out and then Paul, replacing him with her fiancé. It's even possible her fiancé was part of the import business and that's how she met him, isn't it?"

"So now you've added Melody's fiancé to the suspect list?"

The question was no sooner out of her mouth, than the rationale of what Tom said became clear to her. "No. No, I don't think you're right about Melody," she said, though her words lacked their former firm conviction. "But if you are right, we don't have much time to figure out what Melody, or Melody and her fiancé, are up to, do we?

"I've got a hunch about Hector that might go a long way toward telling me whether you, Dave, and he are right about Melody or whether I am. I'm going to follow Hector's advice and talk to her as soon as I get Dave to do a little job for me."

"What do you want him to do?"

"I want him to find out if Hector owns an old SUV."

🏠🏠🏠🏠🏠🏠🏠🏠🏠🏠🏠

"Not exactly," Dave said.

"What an ambiguous answer." Regan frowned as she held her cell phone to her ear with her shoulder.

"I'm looking at my computer screen right now checking vehicle registration and it says your pal Hector Gonzales owns two vehicles, both old. He has a '91 green Chevy Lumina — amazing that thing still runs — and a '99 Chevy truck, color: indigo. The witness was driving in the other direction and admitted to being terrified when she saw what happened, thought the SUV was going to cross the road and take her out, and said she covered her face with her arms, so yeah, it's possible what she saw only from the front was a truck and not an SUV.

"Now me, I'd have been able to come up with at least a partial license number. She called 9-1-1 real fast after the accident. Who knows, maybe her cell phone was handy, like already in her hand and that's why she didn't get the best look at the vehicle. Or since she's a woman, that could explain why she doesn't know her vehicles."

"I have another idea, Dave," Regan pronounced testily. "Perhaps since she wasn't a trained cop like you, she was shocked, it was dark, and she was genuinely frightened, and then more concerned about Melody and her fiancé than looking at the hit and run vehicle, and the fact that she is a woman had nothing to do with anything."

"Could've happened that way," Dave chuckled.

He had been needling her and she had missed it. He got to chalk up a point in their ongoing teasing battle, but it was a small price to pay, considering the favor he was doing her by looking up information about Hector's autos without anything from her other than a request.

"So, what's the deal with this guy. Why are you so curious? You gonna' tell me or should I ask Tom?"

"Quid pro quo for your information, is it?"

"Always."

"I'll tell you; you don't have to ask Tom. Hector Gonzales was a business partner of Paul Valentine's, and you do know what I mean by them being in business together, don't you?"

"Old news."

"You're going to like this. According to Hector, Melody forced him out, and Hector thinks she took his place in the operation."

"What we suspect."

"He's had it in for her ever since."

"Are you ever gonna' tell me something juicy?" Dave made a big deal of sighing loudly.

"Hector approached Tom about going into business with him …"

"Go on."

"We had dinner with him last night to discuss his proposition. He tried to convince us we could turn the garage on our new property into a grow site."

Dave laughed out loud. "And I thought you were about to offer up some good stuff. Your Hector guy is small time and unless you and Tom bought his plan, ancient history."

"You needn't worry about us. The thing is he really has it in for Melody. I think he may be the hit and run driver. Is there a way to find out if Hector's truck is being repaired or has damage to the right front?"

"There's already a bulletin out to repair shops in the greater Bay Area and inland for a hundred miles about an

SUV, van, or truck, dark in color with damage to the right front. If your Hector guy takes his truck anywhere reputable for repair, the authorities will be notified. Nothin' yet."

"That's too bad. I want to approach Melody with the sort of proposition Hector made to us about doing some growing and see how she reacts. Giving her the identity of her assailant might make her grateful and more talkative."

"That is if your buddy Melody doesn't already know who smashed her because she set it up."

"Yes, Dave." Regan didn't attempt to hide the annoyance in her voice. "Whichever way things go, I'll learn something by her reaction to my news about Hector."

"Is Tom OK about you playing best-buds with a suspected drug lady, 'cause I'm not exactly. But then I know better than to try and talk you out of anything. I can hear you now, 'I'm a big girl, Dave, and you're being too protective.' You two still have that security guard around?"

"We do. He's not noticeable, but Tom assures me he's still on the job and we haven't had any more incidents at home or work."

"Good. Ya know, if I thought your Melody was just a small-time grower, I wouldn't care what you did with her, but we think she's big time; and once you start playing with the big boys, well, overprotective or not, be careful. Have public meetings, things like that. Don't try to put her in a box; if you get anything from her, bring it to me and let me and the FBI figure out what to do with her."

"Yes, Dave."

"Hey Regan, I do appreciate you telling me that Hector has it in for Melody. It's within the realm of possibility that you're right about him being the one who whacked her and her guy, even if you probably aren't."

"Why Dave, did you just pay me a compliment?"

"I wouldn't go that far ..."

She cut him off with, "Yes, you did," and hung up before he could quibble.

"How is James feeling? Is he doing well?" Regan asked as the opening lines in her phone call to Melody.

"He's doin' much better. His head has almost stopped achin' and he says he can think again."

"Wonderful. I've been doing some thinking as well ..."

"Yeu're not backin' out of the 17th are yeu?" Melody's voice was full of alarm.

"No, not at all. In fact, I'd like to talk to you about what I'd like to say on the 17th. I know you have something written, but I'd like to welcome everyone in my own words first, if I may."

"That would be wonderful, Regan."

"Since I never knew Chloe, I hope you'll help me with what to say about her. I'd like to see a picture of her, too, so I have a better sense of who she was. You can't come here right now, what with taking care of James and all, so I'll come to you, if that's OK. What's your address and what's a good time for me to stop by and talk?"

Regan was fully aware she was going against Dave's instructions, but she wasn't concerned. She still was seventy to eighty percent certain Melody wasn't the woman the authorities sought, and even if she was, Regan was one-hundred percent certain Melody posed no threat to her, especially at a home meeting and before the 17th.

"Yeu are so kind to me. Tomorrow midday would be good for me. I'll give you a wee bite."

Regan put the Los Gatos Hills address Melody gave her into Google Street Maps. She knew a house in that location would be pricey, but she was unprepared for the property photos that popped up.

The house had obviously been photographed from the air in the days before drones and could only be seen from above because it was gated and private, but even without house details, it was obvious the residence sat high enough to sport a commanding view and was terraced to accommodate a huge pool and tennis and basketball courts. Regan saw dollar signs everywhere she moved her cursor.

As she stared at her computer screen, Regan began to appreciate Dave's and Hector's assessment of Melody — she had expensive taste — and questioned how she had the resources to get such a house. Regan dropped the probability that Melody wasn't involved in criminal activity to fifty-fifty and wondered if she was still giving her an undeserved benefit of the doubt.

🏠🏠🏠🏠🏠🏠🏠🏠🏠🏠🏠🏠

Regan couldn't help but calculate how much income it would take to support such an estate while sitting in front of the property's high gate and watching it lollygag open to a dull grinding sound. By the time the gate was fully open, she had dropped the odds favoring Melody's honesty to less than even money.

The only things separating the property from a movie version of a gangland kingpin's house were armed guards, and for all she knew, they were there, hiding discretely behind the manicured shrubbery surrounding the fence or behind the trees lining the drive to the house. Tom's insinuation, that Melody may have met her fiancé doing drug deals, a previously nagging but dismissible idea, seemed suddenly disturbingly sensible.

Regan parked in the shade of a grape arbor that covered the end of the driveway where it broadened and ended at the left side of the house and walked toward the home's entry doors.

Considering the setting and the lead-up to the house, the residence itself was underwhelming. She had been expecting something grand, a newly built McMansion at least or possibly an even more ostentatious house, but what she saw was clearly an older home: a large midcentury modern that appeared to have been built at a time appropriate for its style.

Melody, visible through the floor-to-ceiling window next to the oversized door, greeted her with a wave before she pulled the door open. She smiled broadly and pulled Regan toward her for a hug.

"It's seu good of yeu to come, Regan. Thank yeu for what yeu and Tom are doin'."

Regan had arrived with a plan in mind for how to broach the subject of returning Melody's former property to the use it had when she and Paul owned it, but as soon as she was fully in the house and freed of Melody's grasp, she put her set-up aside for the time being.

The house and its contents were spectacular, worthy of a listing on an historic homes register. Regan was familiar with midcentury architecture and the most prominent architects who created it — she had to be because Millennials and Gen-Xers who were driving sales in the price range where she often worked liked the style — and while she had seen her share of Eichlers, this house was unlike any she knew. She was transfixed by the translucent glass walls that surrounded her, admitting light from every direction.

"I can tell by the look on yeur face, you recognize James's house is special. His parents commissioned Cliff May to build it. Yeu'd think a lass like me, coming from a land of castles and grand ancient houses, might not appreciate a design by the father of the California Ranch House, but yeu'd be wrong.

"I'm fussied-out by my youth and love everything about this place from the dark concrete floors to the skylights. Look around, Regan, the furniture is by the trendsetters of design, teu. That table made of walnut slabs is George Nakashima, the Eames chair is an original Eames chair, red fabric and all, and my favorite is the egg chair by Arne Jacobsen ... or the diamond chair by — I canna' remember his name, but he's known for them."

Melody laughed in her good-humored style, "It's good they built the house and furniture out of sturdy stuff because, by his own admission, James and his brother were wild children who might have destroyed everythin' in the place if it was filled with precious antiques. James loved the house. Fortunately, his brother was more enamored with Cape Cod homes and livin' back east when their parents died in a car smashup, so James bought him out of this house with part of his inheritance."

At the mention of money, Regan was reminded of her purpose in seeing Melody. "I bet that set James back …"

"Well yes, but James's father was holdin' heavy in Apple stock — he worked for the company from the beginn'in', got founder stock when Apple went public, and exercised every option he ever could — seu there was plenty of money teu go around."

Regan mentally checked two questions off her list. Melody might have the expensive taste Hector said she did, but the house wasn't hers; she didn't need to be a drug lord to buy it. Neither did James, she realized with relief — so much for Tom's theory that Melody and James met in a smuggler's cove — since his money was old and from his family.

That didn't rule out Melody and James running a business now, however, to maintain their lifestyle. "Has James followed in his father's footsteps? I mean, is he a Silicon Valley whiz like his father must have been?"

"He's no Steve Jobs, if that's what yeu mean, but I'm sure he would have become an angel investor if Mr. Jobs needed money back then. He has no aptitude for creatin' product or programmin'," she chortled, "his skills are in recognizin' companies that are going teu make money, and in that, he's quite good. He's been well rewarded for his talent by investin' in a number of startup companies that have gone on to become big names."

Melody put a hand on her ever so slightly rounded stomach. "I felt a fluttering; it's the bairn." She was ecstatic.

Regan remembered her reason for seeing Melody was to suggest they become business partners. She planned to ask and then watch Melody's reaction, but from a financial perspective it was getting harder to make a case for Melody — with or without her fiancé — running a drug smuggling operation. After what she had seen, she decided to put off her questioning and hoped with more information she might not need to go there at all.

As they moved through the house, their conversation turned to Chloe, the little girl Melody and Paul had lost. Regan watched her hostess closely as she spoke. Melody had the pain she felt at the loss under control — she was clearly moving forward with her life — but Regan could still see it in the way she occasionally dropped her glance and hear it in the tone of her voice and in the wistful way she spoke of her lost daughter.

Eventually they reached the living room. In a sweet and generous gesture, Melody offered the prized egg chair to Regan and sat shoes off and curled into an egg-chair-wannabe suspended from a high beam. The chair swayed gently as she spoke. The movement seemed to comfort her and she touched her stomach often, rocking her new baby, as it were, as she spoke of the child she would never hold again.

Surely Tom would agree the risk of prison was too high for rewards that weren't needed by such an affluent couple, especially one with a baby on the way. Yes, Tom would see her logic, although Dave might still need more convincing.

Regan chose her words carefully and asked her question

softly. "In case my words fail to paint a clear picture of her and your guests' memories have softened, do you have a picture of Chloe that I could borrow and have blown up to poster size so everyone will be better reminded of her?"

Melody's eyes brimmed with tears; she quickly wiped aside the one that escaped. "Yes, yes, I'll give yeu my favorite before yeu leave. Letting people see her and be reminded of her is a good idea because she is fading, yeu know, even from my memory. Sometimes when I look at that picture, she seems na' quite the way I remember her. The worst is her voice; Regan, I can no longer hear her voice clearly. And then, many, perhaps most of the people comin' didn't know her at all."

"Melody, I know the 17th is the anniversary of her passing, but perhaps, given what you've been through this week, you should reschedule and hold a belated birthday celebration yourself when you are up to it. Tom and I would have no problem with letting you use the property at a later date. I know you're concerned about notifying everyone, but I'll make that my job. Perhaps the ceremony could be smaller and limited to only those who did know your daughter."

Melody's facial expression toughened and her posture stiffened. Regan knew she was imagining it, but it seemed that as Melody raised her chin and shook her hair slightly, her hair became redder. She was the Scottish warrior queen of history as she had been when she marched through a small army of protestors and into Kiley and Associates, an avenging Boudicca ready to destroy those who had hurt her family. But this time there was rage in her demeanor, not just the intimidation that comes with certain knowledge of superiority.

"Many people comin' dinna' know Chloe, but almost all knew Paul. I've not been completely up front with yeu, Regan, and it's time I am. I believe in your kindness and understanding. I know I can tell you everythin' and trust yeu to keep what I say just between us.

"The 17$^{th}$ is as much about Paul as it is about Chloe. I believe Paul and I, our marriage, would have survived the loss of our daughter; we would have grown closer mournin' her, but by the time Chloe died, it was teu late for us.

"When our daughter was diagnosed with Wilms tumor, a cancer of the kidneys, it had spread and her prognosis was na' good. Poor wee thing had to have surgery and chemo, and radiation, even a stem cell transplant."

"I'm so sorry."

"Her treatment pushed us past the limits of what our insurance would cover. We had long arguments with our carrier, but we couldna' get anywhere. We used all our assets, but even with the best care we could afford, she kept gettin' worse. We were out of money with credit cards maxed, our house mortgaged for more than it was worth, and desperate. We would have done anythin' teu save her. Anythin'.

"That's when Paul's childhood friend Hector found us; Hector with his promises of a miracle. He said he knew a religious man who could save Chloe. Hector said he'd seen it happen before even when all hope was lost. He took us to meet Practitioner Fitzwater. The Practitioner said his group could save Chloe and Paul believed in him with his whole heart."

Regan could understand Paul's need to believe and the

effect a man like Practitioner Fitzwater could have on him since she'd seen what a spell-caster the Practitioner could be and felt his charisma first-hand.

"Hector said the Practitioner was too reticent to ask for money himself, but that he spoke for him. Hector told us we needed two-hundred-and-fifty-thousand-dollars teu pay for cluster prayers and then Chloe would be fine.

"Hector's timin' was seu perfect … perhaps I'm jaded by what has happened in my life since then, but I no longer believe his arrival was coincidental. I think he, he and that horrible Practitioner Fitzwater, were in the business of stealin' from those in pain. By my way of seein' things now, they had been workin' their plan all along, waitin' until we were desperate before Hector approached us, waitin' until we couldna' say no."

Melody's whole body shook with remembered rage. "Can you imagine what that was like for us, Regan, bein' told there was a cure for our precious bairn if only we could pay for it and bein' completely out of money?"

"I can't begin to imagine how hard that would be," Regan sympathized.

"Then Hector told us he knew how teu make money, lots of money. He convinced my husband that the Practitioner was completely unaware of what he was proposing and that he only suggested what he did because he and Paul had been in the business in Colombia so he knew they could make his plan work here. Hector said it would be just like old times if we let him use our land teu grow cannabis and that he already had connections to sell what they grew.

"Of course, we knew it was illegal — and if we'd been

able to think straight, we might have asked him how it was that he already had sales connections — but we also knew growin' was highly profitable and the only way we could get the money teu save Chloe.

"Even seu, Paul hesitated before agreein' to Hector's plan. He knew I would worry about what he was gettin' into, but finally he agreed.

"Paul went so far as to tell me that Practitioner Fitzwater's group had agreed to pray for Chloe without payment and said the prayers had started. I knew better. That Fitzwater man would do nothin' for free, but I dinna' say anythin'.

"So Paul lied teu me about his business deal with Hector — he needn't have because I would have agreed teu anythin' as readily as he did — and when I found out, I signed a contract with the devil just like Paul did."

Melody stared straight into Regan's eyes. "You're a mother, aren't yeu? What would yeu have done in my place?"

Regan was sincere when she replied. "I believe I would have done the same thing you and Paul did."

Melody nodded in poignant agreement. "The money rolled in. The prayers were offered. Chloe died anyway. Paul was overwhelmed with loss and blamed himself for dawdlin' before accepting Hector's scheme and agreein' to work with the Practitioner."

Melody paused and pressed her lips together tightly. When she spoke again her voice had hardened. "Tryin' to save our daughter was one thing, continuin' teu do what he was doin' after she died was another. I demanded that he sever all ties with Hector and end his drug traffickin' immediately.

"Marriages sometimes donna' survive the loss of a child,

but as I said, I think ours would have if Paul did what I asked. He said he had cut loose from Hector; it was another lie. He stayed in the business and got in even deeper with Hector and his connections.

"Our credit cards got paid. Our other debt began teu disappear — and seu did I, emotionally at first and then, when I no longer respected him or trusted him, in all ways. I moved out and after a while met James.

"I donna' how to explain it, Regan, but as disheartened as I was by what Paul did after Chloe died, a part of me still loved him, still does. Now he's dead and I want those that kept him ruinin' his life and our marriage teu pay a price for what they did teu him, teu us. Can yeu understand that?"

Regan thought of Gretchen, her associate, sobbing at Paul's loss even after he had treated her so badly. Once Paul Valentine became involved with a woman, he seemed able to maintain quite a hold on them.

"So the 17th is about remembering Chloe, but it's also about causing trouble. I want to get Paul's partners jailed, but if I cana' deu that, at least I hope teu destroy their business. Imagine what will happen, what will be seen, with so many people rushin' all over the place lookin' for treasure? They'll find where grows are happenin', the hidden places for processin' crops, and the secret places where illicit product is kept until it gets moved out teu buyers. They'll find those places and then seu will the law."

With her fiery red hair and her eyes bright, Melody fairly glowed as she thought of what was about to happen on Sunday.

"I knew I was placing yeu at risk of losing the land if the

Feds confiscated it, and I am sorry for that, but I thought yeu'd have a good argument that yeu just bought it and clearly werena' involved with what was found. If the worst happened, I would have reimbursed yeu for what yeu paid for the property."

Regan listened to Melody's tale first with relief, reassured that she wasn't Dave's drug mastermind and then with growing horror at Melody's naivety. Boudicca paid a terrible price for her victory; Melody was playing as risky a game as the Scottish queen.

"Melody, didn't you consider if you pushed Paul's partners, they could be dangerous?"

"Hector and the Practitioner are con men and Hector is at his core a spineless little manipulator, but not one for physical confrontation. Sure, I thought those two might try to intimidate me when they realized I could wreck their business, but truly I dinna' expect real trouble from either of them."

"Suppose you're right about Hector and the Practitioner, if he's part of this, but what about Paul's connections? They could be dangerous people who might come after you." Regan didn't mention the queasy feeling she had in her stomach when she realized those same dangerous people might now aim their attentions at Tom and her.

"Aye, that was my hope."

Melody's smile was cunning, even cruel. "What I was hopin' was that they'd overplay their hand and be so aggressive about tryin' teu stop my plans that they'd make a serious misstep and show themselves."

"The connections Hector spoke of could be Colombian

drug smugglers using the land to process smuggled cannabis and heroin. If you're right about Paul staying in the business, that's who you might be taunting."

"No, Regan, that's na' possible," Melody shook her red curls, "the connection isna' foreign. Neither Paul nor Hector would get involved with the likes of anyone from Colombia. It was those sorts with their brutality and killin' that drove Paul and him out of the old country."

"If that's true, you may be quite mistaken about Hector's capacity for violence. I asked a friend in the police force to see if Hector has a dark SUV. What he discovered is that Hector owns a dark blue truck. If it has a camper shell on it, the witness to your hit and run could easily have confused it with an SUV. Hector may well have been the driver that hit you and James. My friend is working on finding out if Hector's truck has had any recent damage to its front end."

"Yeu really think Hector is the one who smashed us?" Melody was incredulous.

"I think it's extremely likely he is. The only thing is, I think he may not have done it to stop your plans. I've had an opportunity," what a word, Regan thought, "to talk with Hector. From what he said, it doesn't seem like he and Paul were partnering anymore."

"Yeu've talked to Hector?"

"I've done more than that. You're telling me the whole story about what you've done, I better tell you what Tom and I have been up to. We attended a meeting of the prayer group — so yes, I've met the Practitioner — and asked for help with Uncle Harry, a made up relation we said needed their services.

"Tom played believer to my skeptic and we made it clear we were broke. Hector approached Tom about going into the growing business with him in much the same way he reached out to Paul, which is why I think Paul really did sever ties with him; Hector even said Paul told him he had to in order to try and save your marriage."

Melody pressed her hand on her stomach, touching her baby, as a new type of pain washed across her face.

"He insisted Tom not tell me anything because he was afraid I'd be like you and push him out once the business was up and running. Hector hates you, Melody. He blames you for Paul ending their friendship and tossing him out of a lucrative business. That's motive enough for him wanting to hurt you."

"Or the Practitioner sent him," Melody's eyes became mere slits as she mentioned Practitioner Fitzwater.

"Hector insisted the Practitioner was a real-deal healer who never knew what he and Paul were up to."

"He would have to say that teu get yeu and Tom in his clutches, wouldna' he?"

"It's possible, but I'm inclined to believe everything he said, even about the Practitioner never knowing about Paul and him. I think it's more likely Paul forced Hector out just like you wanted him to and now Hector wants back in, which means when he died, Paul was working with someone else."

"You know what it sounds like to me, Regan?" Dave asked with a superior air. "It sounds to me like your new gal-pal out-foxed you big time. She said blah-blah-blah, sobbed at all the right times, clutched her chest like Miss Piggy and said 'Moi' and you bought it. Frankly, I thought you were a better judge of character."

"I am a good judge of character." Regan parsed her words and her silent thoughts carefully. *She may have been in the past* ... "Melody isn't the person the authorities are after now."

It would have been so much easier to tell Dave everything Melody said and ask that he understand — she wished she could — but that would mean betraying Melody's confidence and putting him in a difficult position, so she kept the truth to herself.

"What I did learn, Dave, is that you and a few of your associates, maybe even someone from the FBI, should come to the big event we are hosting on Melody's behalf on

Sunday. It could prove quite interesting and well worth your time."

"Why do you think that?"

"I can't say, exactly."

"So, you want me to accept your faith-based invitation and you want me to drag some people with me, is that it?"

"If that's how you want to think about it." She couldn't resist adding, "What I can tell you about the event is on a need-to-know basis and you don't need to know more than that you should come."

Dave twisted his mouth to one side and chewed on part of his lip. "Sure, I'll be there and I'll ask around to see if anyone else feels like comin' along with me."

Regan pulled him toward her, hugged him, and kissed him on the cheek. He used the back of his hand to wipe away her sign of affection like a small boy who had just been given a peck by his Aunt Flossie.

"So, readin' between the lines, I get that you're pretty scared about this Sunday, aren't you?"

"Terrified."

"Let me put your mind at ease, me and my pals will be carrying."

🏠🏠🏠🏠🏠🏠🏠🏠🏠🏠🏠

Regan may not have told Dave everything, but as soon as she was alone with Tom in his office, she didn't leave out any details with him.

"I'm more sure than ever that Hector is Melody's hit-and-run driver and that his motives were personal, not anything more.

"Melody tossed around Practitioner Fitzwater's name as being in cahoots with Hector to draw Paul and her into an illegal grow scheme, but even she doesn't think the good Practitioner is Hector's selling connection and I believe Hector when he says that the Practitioner didn't know what he and Paul were up to.

"That leaves someone else in the mix. Tom, I'm worried that whoever that is will do something awful on the 17th. I have visions of a band of swarthy Colombians opening fire with AK47s. Oh, and Dave says he and his little band will be armed." Regan started to laugh with full-on gallows humor. "The shootout at the OK Corral comes to mind only with a couple of hundred or so innocent bystanders trapped inside the fence."

"I'm more concerned about the two days remaining before the 17th than the day of," Tom reasoned. "Once the event starts, your imaginings about automatic weapons warfare," he chuckled, "vivid as they are, won't happen because by then there will be no point to it. No, I worry that if the people who have been poking around our house, and doing who-knows-what in the woods, want to frighten us off, they'll strike between now and then.

"I'll ask the security guard I hired to bring along another person for backup and to be extra vigilant at our house, but I have a great idea. In the interest of our safety, we should get out of town."

He smiled one of his most charming grins and his blue eyes twinkled.

"We could go to Carmel for a couple of days and have a romantic getaway. We would disappear and as an added benefit take our minds off what's been happening."

Regan was drawn into his eye's blueness as she always was when he tossed a romantic suggestion at her. She sighed deeply, "Oh, that's so tempting, but you know we can't."

"Next best suggestion, then: let's throw off the bad guys by not being where they'd expect to find us. Let's stay overnight at the office with its reliable security cameras front and back and its excellent alarm system. We can snuggle on my sofa and pretend we're newlyweds."

Regan giggled and even blushed a bit. "I like that idea. I'll slip home and get what we need."

She put out extra water and some dry food in addition to a fresh can of wet chicken and tuna for Harry and their other cat, Sophie. Regan feared Sophie would be so offended by having to eat dry food in the morning that she would probably kill and eat a bird, but Harry wouldn't mind. Then she packed a change of clothing and what they might need for an overnighter in the office.

Regan was pretty sure there was an old TV and CD player tucked away in a storage closet at work so she threw a couple of romantic old movie classics into her purse, too. For good measure, she grabbed a bottle of excellent Riesling and a negligee she hadn't worn for years. If Tom wanted them to be pretend newlyweds, she was game.

Tom did his part, too. He tasked Amanda with picking up the O'Mei takeout Chinese he ordered before she left for the day, dragged the TV and CD player out of storage, feeling sure Regan would bring some movies, and found a couple of cozy blankets stashed in an office cupboard.

They secured the office when the last agent left at 6:30 and by 9:00 Regan and Tom had feasted on hot and sour soup, mushu, and gan pung chicken while they snuggled and watched *An Affair to Remember*, and finished most of the Riesling. It was dark outside and seemed later than it was, but neither was tired enough to suggest trying out the sofa, and neither was willing to do some paperwork separately, not on a night they were trying hard to make a distracting and romantic one.

"I think the speech about Chloe Valentine I want to make on Sunday is almost ready. Usually public speaking is easy for me, but this time it's more complicated. Could I practice on you? It's a short speech; it won't take long to present and you can help me smooth out some of the rough spots." What Regan suggested was hardly romantic, but at least it was something they could do together.

"Sure."

"It's on my laptop. Let's go to my office where I can read it to you and we can make changes easily." They moved across and down the hall, turning on the light in Regan's office when they reached it.

"I feel like a goldfish," Tom said as he closed the outside blinds. "That's better," he said as he settled into one of Regan's guest chairs near the window.

She stood behind her desk and brought the speech up on her computer. "I'll start by thanking everyone for coming."

Tom frowned and cocked his head toward the driveway outside the office.

"Is that a car heading to our parking lot? Darn. Are we going to be busted by one of our agents bringing a client here for a late-night contract signing?" he snickered.

"I'm glad I delayed putting on my powder blue negligee," she laughed.

"You brought a negligee?" Tom raised and lowered his eyebrows expressively, a big grin on his face.

Romantically distracted as they were, neither was aware of the sound of the car returning up the driveway toward the street. But the sound of shattering glass got through to them. The blinds dissipated the force of the thrown rock and kept it from coming very far into Regan's office, but the window shattered completely and fell to the floor in crumbly pieces, and the rock succeeded in punching a good-sized hole in the blinds.

The fireball that followed the rock landed on the chair next to the one where Tom sat. The chair exploded in flames. Fiery tendrils, blue-hot with conflagration, dripped from the cushion onto the floor and spread out in every direction.

"GET OUT!" Tom shouted as he raced to the doorway.

Regan yanked her laptop from its tethering cords and slammed it shut, holding it left-handed against her chest as she rounded the edge of her desk. With her right hand, she grabbed the trunk of the fiddle leaf ficus next to the doorway, a leafy green fixture that had happily grown in its basket since the day she moved into the office, and yanked. The plant upended and its plastic pot came out of the basket. Regan tugged at the plant and loose pot and dragged them from the room.

Tom returned deploying the hose on the red fire

extinguisher from the break room as he ran toward the flames. "Call 9-1-1," he commanded.

Regan dropped her laptop on the reception counter and let go of her rescued tree. She punched in the emergency call on Amanda's landline.

Regan was vaguely aware that there was a small firehouse on Younglove Avenue just a couple of blocks away from the office. She had never seen any firemen hanging around outside it or seen the doors rolled up to show off the fire engines, so she had dismissed it as a relic, but she had barely finished giving the office address to the emergency operator when she heard the foghorn-like blare of an engine from so close by, it must have been coming from that fire station. She vowed she would never again pass the station without saluting it.

A sooty version of Tom grabbed her arm, "I ran out of retardant; we better get outside."

She picked up her laptop as he began pulling her toward the front door. "My tree," she shouted over the crackle of flames and the sound of the engine blasting louder as it turned down their block.

Tom released her arm and picked up the tree by its trunk. It came out of its plastic pot. He hauled it toward the front door, which he gave a push with his shoulder.

Within seconds a fire engine pulled into their driveway and well-trained men scampered off of it. Two rounded the front of the building to where Tom and Regan were standing.

"Anyone left inside?" one bellowed.

"No."

"Are either of you hurt?"

After Tom answered, "No," and the firefighter had shouted for them to move away from the building, waving them back as he did, he disappeared inside.

A couple of firemen disbursed a hose which remained attached to the truck and began pouring water into Regan's office through the broken window. Another firefighter pulled a folded hose down the street to the nearest hydrant and attached it. The firefighter who told them to move re-immerged and helped unfurl the hydrant hose which he and his partner pulled through the open doors.

Regan, Tom, and an ever-growing crowd of onlookers who came down the street from Kelly's, the still-open restaurant in the Swift Street mini-mall, stood in the middle of the street to watch the excitement.

Tom held Regan's tree off the ground. When he realized he still clutched it, he put the dirt end down, pressed it into the asphalt to spread the dirt and balanced it so it remained more or less upright, and took his wife's hand.

Flames shot up through the roofline over what had been Regan's office, but they quickly began to lick lower, giving way to the firefighter's attack and the onslaught of water from two directions. In what seemed like a matter of minutes, the flames disappeared altogether.

One of the counter-people at Kelly's who knew them well because of their frequent coffee forays came up behind Regan and Tom, put a hand on each of their shoulders giving them a loose embrace. "I'm sorry, guys. At least it looks like most of your office is salvageable. How did the fire start?"

"It didn't start," Tom said. "It was started."

"Thank goodness both of you are OK. I may have to

change my mind about you once again, Regan, since I see even in the midst of adversity you saved your tree."

Regan recognized the mocking voice behind her and spun toward her husband and around enough to face a smiling Taylor Bingham looking up at her.

"We were just picking up a late-night snack at Kelly's when we saw the commotion, weren't we, Christopher?"

Taylor inclined her head toward a young green-haired man as she spoke. Regan knew him only too well. He was the most prominent of the protestors who had plagued them and was Regan's primary suspect as the rock thrower who had broken their sliding glass door.

"That's right." He held up a pink pastry box by the strings tied around it. "We got pie."

"You did this! You tried to kill us!" Regan was the closest she had ever been in her life to physically attacking another person; indeed, she would have taken a swing at Taylor or the pie-holder if not that her left hand still clutched her laptop and Tom's tightening grip on her right hand.

Taylor and the green-haired man took a step back in unison. "Whatever are you talking about?" Taylor protested with a shrill voice that was full of childlike innocence like it had been in Regan's office days before. "Get a grip. Given your mental state now I wonder, did you save your tree, or was that your husband's doing?"

Regan struggled to break free of Tom's restraining grip.

Taylor took her companion's arm and ushered them through the crowd in the direction of the parking lot by Kelly's.

Tom craned his neck, watching as the green-haired man

unlocked the door of a small older car and he and Taylor got into it. They used the back parking lot entrance to drive away, avoiding turning toward the street and Tom's watchful glance.

Once he was confident that Regan wasn't going to run after Taylor, Tom let go of her hand and put the trunk of the ficus tree into it. He started for the front door of the office, but was stopped by one of the firefighters.

"You best not go inside, sir, until we've inspected the building for safety. From the look of you, I assume you were inside when the fire started, is that right? What can you tell me about how the fire started? Did you notice a spark from an electrical outlet; did you drop a cigarette?"

"The fire started when someone tossed in what I expect you'll discover during your investigation was a Molotov cocktail-like device."

"Sir?"

"Check it out. In the meantime, I'll take responsibility for myself and my safety. I need some things from my office which is across the hall and forward from where the fire was. That area should be perfectly safe."

"Tell me what you need and I'll see what I can do, but you can't go inside," the firefighter was unwavering.

Tom and he were still negotiating when Dave and his wife, Sandy, drove into the parking lot across the street and took the space vacated by Taylor and the green-haired man. Sandy trotted across the parking lot, ran down the street, and forced her way through the crowd until she reached Regan.

"Oh my goodness, are you and Tom okay?"

"We're fine," Regan said as she gave a hug back to her

friend.

Dave was close behind. "Working late, were you?" he asked.

"No. We thought it would be a good idea to stay here for the night instead of going home. We'll go back inside as soon as the firefighters give us an all-clear."

"Cleanup will take longer than you think," Sandy said. "You two are coming to our house and using the guest room tonight."

"How did you know about us, about the fire?" Regan queried.

"The same officer who interviewed you after Valentine's body was found in your back yard told me. He just came on duty and heard the fire alarm report. Seems he recognized the Kiley and Associates name and remembered that was you guys. He likes you two for some reason and thought you might need to see some friendly faces." Dave's smile teased, but his hug told a different story.

"So I'm not officially workin' 'cause it's Saturday and I don't work weekends — besides, for now your office mess is one for the fire department, not the police department — but I'd sure like to hear what happened. In your own words." Dave poured orange juice in his glass and waited to see which of his friends would speak first.

Regan did. "Can we file a police report with you even though it's Saturday?"

"And what would that police report say, exactly?"

"It would say Taylor Bingham and her flunky, Christopher — that was what she called him, wasn't it, Tom — fire-bombed our office last night and tried to kill us."

Dave took a sip of his juice and raised his eyebrows.

"I'm not as sure as Regan is that they were trying to kill us," Tom added, "but she's right about the fire-bomb."

"If it landed on the chair you were sitting in instead of the one next to you ..." When the full realization of what she was saying hit her, Regan couldn't finish her sentence.

"But it didn't and Tom wasn't hurt," Sandy comforted her.

"You think whoever did what they did last night was only trying to scare you, Tom?" Dave asked. "Why don't you think they were trying to kill you?"

"It was after hours," Tom reasoned. "They probably thought the office was empty."

"But you heard a car go down our driveway. Our cars were parked in back so our attacker had to have seen them. Taylor might not know they belonged to us, but she had to know someone was in the office."

"Regan's got a point," Dave said.

"Not only that, we turned the lights on in my office when we went there from your office. If the lights were only on in your office on the other side of the building, well maybe the fire bomber could have assumed the cars belonged to someone who was just using the parking lot, but that wasn't the case."

"She's almost thinkin' like a real detective," Dave smiled. "How many windows you think there are next to the driveway?"

Regan tried to visualize the office from outside and began using her fingers to count out her memory.

"That was a rhetorical question," Dave stopped her. "My point is they picked the one window with a light on in the room. If it's up to me, I'm leaning to harm, not scare." Dave started laughing. "Imagine that, me agreeing with Regan. Is there some sort of cosmic shift goin' on I missed?"

Regan rephrased her complaint. "OK then, Taylor Bingham and Christopher ... Doe, since I don't know his last name, firebombed Kiley and Associates on the night of April 15th at 9:00 p.m. That's how the police report should read."

"Just when I thought there was hope she was learning how an investigation works," Dave groaned dramatically. "Even an over-eager news reporter wouldn't convict anybody without a trial, especially not someone like Taylor Bingham, winner of a county-wide award for Environmentalist of the Year, Woman of the Year, and a whole string of other awards, and pillar of the local save our forests movement that she is."

"Throw in an 'allegedly' or two if you must, the facts remain the same. She's been annoyed at me for letting Melody hold her April 17th commemoration. She was there, Dave, within minutes of when the flames started. Doesn't that prove she did it?"

"It doesn't prove diddly-squat. She said she was hungry. Kelly's is a popular spot for baked goods. She could have been buyin' dessert just like she said. So she doesn't want a bunch of non-tree-huggers messin' with her woods for a day. She's passionate about her trees, but no one has ever accused her of being a nut job and she's never so much as taken a swing at anyone with that big stick she carries more often than not. You really think she'd try to kill you to keep her trees and the little baby bunnies that live in the woods happy? That's a case I wouldn't want to take to court."

Regan toyed with blurting out, "Maybe Christopher did it on his own," but she saw an immediate hole Dave would find in that reasoning: Did he drop Taylor off to wait in line while he did the deed? If the green-haired man was the fire bomber, Taylor had to be in on it, too.

"I could almost make a case for the car the green-haired man was driving tonight being the same one that I saw racing away from our house the night our slider had a rock thrown through it. Tonight, another rock was thrown preceding the firebomb. Doesn't that seem like a pattern?" Tom asked. "I like them as suspects for our mayhem, if not for attempted murder."

"Suppose Tom's right. Suppose Taylor was just trying to scare us like he said. Maybe she thought we'd get out of the building before the fire got out of hand, which is what we did. Christopher got people to picket our office building — you can't believe Taylor wasn't the real organizer there, can you? — maybe what happened tonight was just a step up from that."

"That's a lot of maybes, even for you, Regan. 'Maybe' whoever did this has a better motive because she's part of a bigger picture than you're seeing. I don't want to speculate on whether or not whoever tossed that fireball in your window thought you could get out or not. If it was a device like Tom thinks — and I do think the fire forensic team will discover it was — those things don't work like a log accidently rolling out of a fireplace. They're designed to throw accelerant everywhere and to burn hot and hard and not be easy to control. No, the fact they targeted the one window with a light on, I think the intent was to do great bodily harm or worse.

"And you know who would have no qualms about doing that? Colombian drug runners, that's who. Yep," he nodded, "Colombians and people who associate with them." Dave held out a hand and wiggled his fingers, "That's maybe overstating, or maybe not. Fifty–fifty. What we think is you've got neighborhood talent who are playing patty-cake with drug runners and maybe asked them to handle you two.

"For all we know our local may have told the tosser to just mess with you enough to take your mind off business for a while, but he went over the top because that's how things are done in Colombia."

Tom fell silent and was uneasy; Regan was having nothing of what Dave suggested.

"Colombians, cartels, and local drug lords, oh my," Regan used Dorothy's 'lions, tigers and bears, oh my' pacing in the *Wizard of Oz* for her words. "Or it could simply be Taylor behind everything, Taylor who knows my car and has been in my office more than once so she knows which one it is."

"Can you think of any other females, maybe ones with a likely history of playing with drug dealers, who know your car and have been to your office, Regan? 'Cause that's where I think you should be lookin' for who did this."

"You're back to Melody, aren't you?"

"I never left her. You're the ones trying to put your little tree-hugger in the mix." Dave spoke without agitation or anger. "She know what you drive, Regan?"

*Of course she does; I was just at her house.*

"She ever been to your office?"

*Yes, she has.*

"I take it by your silence and the fact that you don't have a snappy comeback about how off I am, that you're sitting here wondering about her.

"Don't bother to tell me she wasn't the one who threw the firebomb. She probably wouldn't be. She'd call her Colombian thug-friends and say, 'Could you do me a little favor, Darlins? Could you scare my dear friend Regan so she'll finally give up on this 17th ting like I always planned?'" Dave tried to impersonate Melody as he spoke, but instead of a Highland accent, his impression was delivered in an Irish brogue.

"It's such a neat package, Regan, right down to Tom's pal Hector being the one who did the hit and run on Melody and her boyfriend, the nice soft hit where nobody was hurt bad, but she could play the loving caretaker who couldn't leave her man, and dump the 17th on you two. Yeah, we checked. Hector's truck hasn't been seen since the accident and some of his neighbors said it had a camper shell on it."

Tom made an attempt to lay out the facts and connections clearly in case he had missed something. "If I have this lined up right, Dave, you believe Melody is the rumored female involved in this drug conspiracy, and that she's in partnership with some very scary individuals from Colombia."

Tom rubbed his chin thoughtfully, "I wonder, could Hector still be in on it with her? Could he have been one of the men who was on our hillside and broke our slider? Regan, he's got a slight build like the men we saw, although ..."

"Care to make a bet, guys?" Dave challenged. "I say the FBI arrests her and Hector within a couple of weeks."

Regan's mind churned. Dave saw everything through the prism of Melody's guilt, but Melody was innocent. She had to find a way to convince Dave, since he already had the propensity to make himself part of the investigation, to get his fellow law enforcement officers to look elsewhere for their drug queen. If she couldn't figure how to do it, she might have to tell Dave everything Melody told her, and that would include her past short-time involvement with Hector and Paul's growing.

If she told Dave everything, Melody might not be charged for current crimes, but she could be for past crimes. It was true that Melody was guilty, but to Regan's way of thinking, in the lead-up to losing Chloe, what Melody did was understandable. How could she let Melody be punished for doing everything she thought she must to save her child?

Regan couldn't break her confidence; she couldn't rob Melody of a fresh start with her new baby. She had to find another way to dissuade Dave. She hit on a weak distractor.

"If Hector is in business with Melody and a bunch of Colombians, why would he try to get us involved too?"

"Think about it, Regan," Dave said. "So you'd be as guilty as they are. What better way to make sure you'd let them use what's now your land than by making you partners in crime?" He looked extremely pleased after giving his explanation.

Tom shook his head. "No, Dave. I'm pushing to see it that way, but it's not tracking. Hector came to us because he thought we needed money to treat Uncle Harry. His connection with us is by way of Practitioner Fitzwater. He saw partnering with us as an opportunity he couldn't miss to get back into the growing business. That would mean he and Melody — and any other nefarious characters you want to add to the gang — had parted company."

"Fine. You know what that means? It means Melody took over the business exclusively after her hubby offed himself and is in cahoots with Colombians all by herself."

"If that's true," Tom wondered out loud, "if Melody controlled growing — with or without external drug runners as partners — the most reasonable thing for her to do was to never have sold the property to us or anyone else. It would have been easy for her to keep the land. With Paul's suicide, she could have taken the property off the market, and if anyone wanted to know why, simply said it no longer needed to be sold as part of a divorce settlement."

A relieved Regan smiled appreciatively at her husband. *Thank goodness for his logical mind.* "Of course. If Melody was using the property for a criminal drug business, that's exactly what she would have done." Regan pounced, "Two things are obvious, Dave. First, Hector wanted back in because he was no longer part of the operation, and second, Melody sold her land to us because she isn't part of any growing business ... or any other kind of illicit business." She needn't say more; Melody's secrets were safe, at least with her and at least for now.

Dave wasn't ready to let Melody off. "If your gal-pal isn't the woman running things, then who is she?"

"Maybe the rumor about a female behind whatever's happening on our new property is just that: a rumor." She wanted to add, *perhaps it got started when Melody was part of the operation with Paul and Hector,* but of course she couldn't. "If you want to make any bets, I bet you'll have a lot more information after Sunday. Please convince your law enforcement associates to wait until then before they make any moves."

12

Tom and Regan slept at home on the night of the 16th, or at least they were in their own bed that night. Tom's security guards were around and Regan was pretty sure Dave had recruited some backup people, as well. They were expected to feel secure; of course they didn't.

Tom lost his battle to stay awake at about 3:30, the book he was trying to read having fallen on his chest again, but this time failing to rouse him when it landed.

Regan sat vigil in the living room drinking cup after cup of Earl Grey with Sophie — who uncharacteristically for a cat at night hadn't moved for hours — and Harry, the cat deemed to be a dog in a cat's body for Hector's benefit, remained as awake as she did. She squinted through the glass wall at the back of their house expecting to see a revenant Paul Valentine or worse, dark-clad quasi-military types from a foreign land, but the night remained quiescent.

At least it did until 4:30 or so; Regan didn't bother to note the time when the first light appeared by Paul's house. Soon the intensity and amount of light at the empty house increased until the night glowed with radiance equal to a small star.

She and Tom kept a telescope on a tripod in the living room. Sometimes they took it outside like they did when Haley's Comet was visible for the only time it would be in their lifetime, but usually it remained indoors where they used it to spy on ships moving in Monterey Bay or to have a close-up look at a gorgeous bird sitting in one of their trees. On the morning of the 17th, she swung it in the direction of their dead neighbor's house.

The dark-clad figures she feared were there in numbers, but instead of weapons, they were carrying large boxes, some big enough to require two people to move them, and transferring them from tractor tows coming out of the woods and from the small out-building that stood as a sentinel to the property into waiting trucks and vans encircling the area. They used the lights in the open garage and from the vehicle headlights to illuminate the area for the workmen.

Regan raced to the kitchen phone with Harry in hot pursuit. She picked it up to dial, and Harry, who was not allowed on the kitchen counters, jumped up next to the phone, undisciplined for his indiscretion, to encourage her. She was still trying to decide if it was more appropriate to call Dave or 9-1-1, when a flashlight's beam appeared in the courtyard, the slider separating the courtyard from their kitchen moved quietly, and her heart all but stopped.

"Don't panic, Regan," Dave, dressed completely in black and with a ski hat pulled down over his hair and black-face covering even the bottoms of his ears said, "it's only me."

"Dave, there are lights and men ..."

"We know. Agents are moving in. Looks like the bad guys' hand got forced."

"You were outside guarding us?"

He shrugged, "Couldn't not be."

"I want to watch." Regan moved past Dave back toward the living room and the ever-faithful Harry meowed at Dave and followed her.

When Regan peered through the telescope this time what she saw was a highly orchestrated surrounding of the package carriers by armed men. Most workers dropped their boxes and raised their hands as weapons were pointed at them.

Regan's attention was drawn to one suspect in particular. The slim man had longish hair which hung down behind his beanie, and although the light was considerably less than daylight, as he slipped backward in what appeared to be an innocent stumble his beanie came off and his head was fully highlighted by a truck headlight. Regan thought his hair had a green cast to it.

"Dave, the green-haired man is there! Look!" she squealed as she relinquished the scope to him.

Dave used his sighted eye to peer through the scope's eyepiece. "They got someone all right. I don't see green hair, though."

"It's hard to see." She forced Dave away from the scope for another look. Two agents wearing vests proclaiming they were FBI had arms entwined on either side of a struggling hatless man with longish hair. His hair was dark and he sported a noticeable paunch.

"That's not him. You must have jiggled the scope when you looked."

"I didn't," Dave protested.

Regan swung the scope to take in the rest of the scene.

The beanie-less man whose hair appeared greenish was nowhere in sight.

"I don't see him now. Dave, he's gone; I think he got away."

"No one got away, Regan. Your eyes are playing tricks on you. Lack of sleep'll do that to you. Lack of sleep and an overactive imagination, which we know you have."

Tom appeared, rubbing his eyes as he came into the living room. "What's happening?" he asked.

"We're watching a bust," Dave replied. "It looks like the threat of tomorrow was too much for your drug lords so they decided to move out tonight. Not too bright of them. We were expecting something like that and ready. FBI and some of our guys are mopping up as we speak."

"Tom, the green-haired man was there."

Tom noticed the tense she used. "Was there?"

"Regan's seeing things."

"He was there, but he's not now. He must have gotten away in the confusion."

"There was no confusion, Regan. The FBI guys are pros. No one got away."

Regan awoke with a start at 8:30 on Sunday morning. She planned to be up, ready, and at the Valentine property by 8:00 to welcome the Practitioner and his group who were due then, but after such a late and nail-biting night, she overslept.

Tom was gone, however, no doubt filling in admirably. It

was probably better that she not be there, she rationalized her tardiness, because they had decided to continue their theatrics about Uncle Harry with Practitioner Fitzwater and Hector for at least one more day, and Tom could still play a man with a need — an ally — while she might be seen as a detractor.

Regan took her cup of coffee to the living room, rested it on a nearby table, and put both hands on the telescope. It was still trained on the house, or more precisely the area where the smugglers' vehicles had been and where arrests were made. She moved it slightly and Practitioner Fitzwater's group came into view.

They were a colorful group, each dressed in a different brightly-colored solid hue. She looked for Hector and found him in his multi-colored garb next to the Practitioner, who was dressed in a solid white robe which fell to his feet.

Another micro-move of the scope brought Tom into focus. He was at the back of the pack, sitting cross-legged on a blanket on the ground. He was wearing jeans — she was sure of that — Tom would wear jeans if he was going to an outdoor meeting in the woods. His top was problematic. It was light in color, but beyond that she couldn't decide with any certainty if it was his earth-colored sweater with a zipper at the neck, his light cream-colored windbreaker, or his pale tan suede jacket zipped closed. Was she sure about his pants because she could see the color clearly or had what she saw been colored by her expectations?

It was a bright morning, filled with sunshine, and still she couldn't be sure of the subtler colors of Tom's clothing like she was of the rainbow-bright Prayers or the Practitioner's blindingly white robe.

Maybe Dave was right. Probably Dave was right. How could she have seen green hair at night relying only on a truck headlight for illumination? She hated to admit it because she had been so sure, but her anger at Taylor Bingham and the green-haired man for what she believed they had done to her office the night before probably did influence what her tired eyes thought they saw last night.

Dave might be right, but she wasn't going to share her conclusion with him any time soon — a confession like that would be tossed at her for years to come.

She showered and dressed in a style reminiscent of Tom's, wearing jeans, a pale green jacket over a long-sleeved white tee shirt, and low-heeled booties. Once she put on a touch of mascara and some lip gloss, she pulled her auburn hair into a pony-tail and pronounced herself ready to join her husband and the power Prayers.

Her final move before leaving the house was to print out the short welcoming speech she had prepared for the masses of people due to arrive in another couple of hours to commemorate Chloe Valentine's birthday. She folded the single page and put it in her jacket pocket.

Regan parked her car with others well back from the prayer group and slipped toward them as quietly as she could. She sat down next to Tom and gave him a light kiss on the cheek by way of greeting.

"Interesting morning," he whispered in her ear as he returned her peck. "I'll tell you about it later."

The Practitioner's arms were raised skyward and his eyes closed tightly. He radiated an almost palpable charisma just as he had at The Bigfoot Museum that was not diminished by the scale of his outdoor surroundings. He intoned words Regan struggled to understand. His voice was clear and forceful. It wasn't that she couldn't hear him, it was that his words made no sense to her.

Tom cupped his hand over his mouth as he again whispered into her ear. "He's speaking in an ancient language only he understands."

She turned her head toward him and opened her mouth. Tom winked at her.

Regan returned her attention to the Practitioner when he pronounced something she did recognize. In the midst of his gibberish, he said, "Chloe Valentine."

Practitioner Fitzwater dropped his arms to his sides and returned to English. "Dearly departed Chloe Valentine needs to move to the next plane. There she will live much as she would on earth, knowing joy, sorrow, happiness, sadness, love, and loneliness just as we do here, but she will feel no pain as she works toward eternal salvation.

"She was just a child when she left us and, therefore, not fully prepared for her journey. She needs our prayers and guidance to help her move forward.

"Let us offer up a prayer for Chloe Valentine," the Practitioner chanted as he raised his arms upward. The congregation followed his lead. "Dearest child, Chloe ..." Her name seemed to echo as it was repeated by the congregant Prayers.

"Stop it, yeu devil! Stop it, all of yeu! Yeu have na' right teu steal her name. Leave my bairn in peace!"

Melody, red hair flying behind her like a burst of rocket

flame, charged past Regan and Tom on her fist-raised charge at the Practitioner. Neither had to be told what to do; Regan and Tom were on their feet rushing to stop her before she attacked.

Hector threw himself in front of Practitioner Fitzwater protectively, cowering as he raised his arms over his head to deflect her first blow.

"Don't you touch him!" Hector screeched.

Tom caught Melody's right wrist before her fist made contact with either man; Regan grabbed Melody's left arm as she pivoted to aim a blow with that fist.

"Let me go!" Melody twisted and struggled as her rage gave way to tears. They held her firmly until her legs buckled and she sank to her knees sobbing. Her head fell forward and was obscured by masses of curls, red-gold in the morning light.

"Yeu have no right, yeu have no right," she sobbed.

Hector straightened up and seemed ready to strike his own blow at the downed and defeated woman at his feet.

Practitioner Fitzwater stopped him with a single touch to his shoulder. "Leave her, Hector. She's in pain. She needs our love, not the back of our hand." He stooped toward Melody, "We only seek to help."

Hector's protective temper dissipated as the Practitioner spoke. "You and Paul waited too long and let doctors put too much poison in your daughter. If only I had found you sooner and you let the Practitioner and his Prayers do their work …"

"Hector, stop," Practitioner Fitzwater spoke firmly. "Nothing that we do is certain. But I hope that we have done enough today that the child may rest now. I would like to think of Chloe and Paul hand-in-hand moving to the next plane. Now it is time for us to leave this poor woman in peace."

Regan dropped down next to Melody and cradled her as she continued wailing, her body racked by piteous sobs.

"How could he come here today?" Melody asked between rushes of tears. "Why would he deu such a thing?"

"We gave him permission, Melody. I was going to tell you, but then when you weren't coming, I didn't say anything. After your suspicions about the Practitioner and Hector — I'm so sorry — I didn't think you were right, but what if you were? I wanted them here when all hell broke loose."

Melody raised her head to look at Regan, a wan smile on her lips. "Yeu expected hell teu break loose? Well then, good for yeu for invitin' him."

"I didn't expect you. What are you doing here?" Regan asked.

"I was on my way teu yeur house teu relieve yeu in pearson when I saw yeur car parked out by the road and the gate open. I thought I better see if yeu and Tom were already here. I dinna' expect … I made quite a scene dinna' I?"

"You did, but we learned something because of you."

"What's that?"

"Their reaction proves the Practitioner didn't know what Paul and Hector were doing and that when Hector says he believes in Practitioner Fitzwater, he means it. He was willing to take a blow for the good Practitioner."

Regan smiled as she spoke and an impish Melody said, "What a shame yeu and Tom were seu swift. I'd have enjoyed flattening that little man."

Melody turned somber. "Regan, what he said: deu yeu think in his mind he really was tryin' teu help us?"

"I'd hardly say his motives were pure — he wanted to make money in the deal and he wasn't worried about leading you down an illegal path — but yes, since he seems to believe in the Practitioner, I think he was."

Melody recovered quickly. By the time she explained that James was doing well and knowing what an important day today was for her, insisted she leave him and come to Chloe's remembrance, Melody had completely regained her composure.

"I'll be deuin' the talkin'. I can't wait to see what I set in motion," Melody said.

"You don't know about last night? Of course you don't." *How could you?* "Paul's partners got spooked just like you hoped and tried to move out their operation. The FBI and local police were waiting. They got them, Melody. You already got what you wanted."

As the noon hour neared, people began arriving, some on horseback, most on foot. Regan noted the presence of children and was especially aware of one thin girl who wore a pink band on her bald head. Melody was quick to hug the child's parents, and Regan wondered if they had met while sharing their struggles with childhood cancer.

Melody moved through the crowd, greeting people as they arrived. Regan even saw her engaged in an exchange with Hector. They had a fairly long conversation and Melody held herself stiffly upright during it, but before she moved on,

Melody extended her hand to him. He grasped her hand in both of his.

Knowing her, Regan could imagine Melody's benevolence as they spoke. As she watched the expression on Hector's face, she thought Melody might even be thanking him for trying to help Chloe. She wondered what emotions the man who likely hit James and Melody with his truck was feeling and if he confessed his crime or kept it to himself.

Regan heard Taylor's voice before she saw her. The woman had an uncanny ability to appear as if forming in a whiff of smoke, and to Regan it seemed as if she was always sneaking up on her.

"I see you are going through with this woods-trampling event," Taylor spoke with a mixture of annoyance and resignation. "I assume now that you've had a chance to cool off after your fire and your matching outburst, and I'm not in any danger being here. You'll notice, however, that unlike the other night, I have my trusty and weighty walking stick with me just in case you overreact to my presence."

Regan could feel her Irish rising; she used verbal scorn and sarcasm to keep it in check. "And I assume you're here to admit no matter what you do, you don't rule the woods after all. Or am I wrong? Are you here to offer your blessings?"

"Hardly. I intend to ask these despoilers to be mindful and try to minimize the damage they do by staying close by this area, which has already been ruined."

Regan scanned the growing crowd looking for the green-haired man. There was still a possibility she had seen him last night and that he had been arrested as Dave promised. If he had, she was sure Taylor would have heard by now.

"I don't see your sycophant, Christopher. Did he eat too much pie and have a rough Saturday night?"

Taylor didn't react to her harsh words. "No. No, he had a fine Saturday night, a productive one, in fact." She softened her tone. "You've just missed seeing him. He's here somewhere getting reacquainted with a friend, I believe."

*He's a free man. That clinches it. I was imagining seeing him last night.*

"Regan, after today, if what you've told me in the past about your desire to be a proper steward of the land is true, don't you agree we should try to bury the hatchet? Christopher would still make a fine tenant for your house; I ask you to please reconsider him. He could be helpful to you and I know you'll find him a pleasant enough young man when he's working with you instead of against you."

Taylor chuckled and touched Regan's arm like they were best friends. "As an added bonus, you'll find my largesse would come along with his residency and a properly placed word from me here or there could garner sales for you and your company. We have no reason to go on as adversaries when we could work together so well for common goals."

Melody stepped up on a low platform erected for the day and began welcoming people using a handheld mic.

"Do give my proposal some thought." Taylor smiled as broadly as she might have if Regan had handed her keys to the house and told her Christopher was welcome. "Now if you'll excuse me, Regan, duty calls."

The elfin woman, who next to tall, commanding Melody seemed almost no bigger than many of the youngsters present, managed to dislodge the mic and began speaking before a startled Melody could protest.

"I have just a few words for you before Ms. Buchanan welcomes you. Consider how blessed we are to have this amazing wilderness in our lives, this forest which is home to so many grand free animals such as deer, raccoons, wood rats, bobcats, coyotes, opossums, skunks, foxes," she paused to take a breath, "feathered creatures such as turkeys, hawks, ravens, owls, and other birds too numerous to mention, and thanks to the caring people who have donated to the Land Trust to build a safe passage under Highway 17 connecting our land with other wild spaces, an increasing population of magnificent cougars ..."

*She sounds like an Academy Award winner thanking her minions.* Regan tuned her out, finding it more interesting to continue looking for her unlikely future tenant. When she spotted the green-haired Christopher, she couldn't have been more surprised than if she discovered him blowing her kisses.

He stood away from the crowd engrossed in a very intimate heads-together conversation with Hector.

Dave let her know he came — Regan wasn't sure he would after last night's arrests — with a tap on the shoulder just as Taylor finished her speech and returned the microphone to Melody. She gave him hurried instructions: "Dave, quick, look over there," she pointed with her whole arm and waved her index finger toward where the green-haired man and Hector were having their cozy conversation, "they're in cahoots!"

"Who is?"

"Hector and the ..." she turned to make sure she was aiming toward the duo. Hector stood alone, his feet apart and his arms folded over his chest as he listened to Melody. "He was there a minute ago."

"Who was?"

"Christopher. The green-haired man."

"It looks to me like your rainbow-bright tie-dyed suspected hit-and-run driver and illicit growing suggester is all alone, Regan. I don't see any cahoots happening. I do see your green-haired man standing with your little stick-wielding pal talking to Tom, though.

"Tom looks kinda' uncomfortable. Shall we go rescue him?"

Regan was two steps ahead of Dave by the time they reached Tom. Uncomfortable wasn't a strong enough word to describe what Tom's expression told her.

"Regan. Dave," Tom beamed. He spoke like an overboard man who couldn't believe his luck at stumbling across long-lost friends who happened to be floating by in a life-raft.

"Your husband has graciously told us he'll talk to you about renting the house to Christopher," Taylor clucked. "Your husband is such a lovely man."

"Again, Mr. Kiley, I am sorry if our protest inconvenienced you. It's just that I feel so passionate sometimes, I get carried away." Christopher lowered his head in the bow of a respectful supplicant.

"Well, we're finished here; we'll be going now," Taylor took the green-haired man's arm. "Come, Christopher."

As Christopher looked up again, Regan noticed a scratch above his right eyebrow. It was camouflaged somewhat because it paralleled the top of his eyebrow hairs, but it looked like a deep cut. She hadn't noticed it when she last saw him on the night of their office fire, and the redness and slight swelling surrounding it suggested it was fresh.

Dave said nothing after the two left, but Regan was sure her well-trained and observant friend noticed the cut, too. She wondered if he had the same thought she had: *is that from last night in the woods?*

All that had happened in the last three days had caught up with them. Tom was tired — the bags under his blue eyes proved it — and Regan was exhausted. The sun had barely set and they hadn't had dinner yet, but she was already in pajamas.

"What do you think?" she asked. "Take-n-bake pizza, microwaved leftover lasagna, or grilled-cheese sandwiches? That's all I'm up for doing. And if you want salad, you'll have to make it."

"I do, and I'll try, but we better have a bag of pre-washed lettuce in the fridge or," he teased, "I can't take on such a big commitment, especially if you expect me to pick the main course, too."

Regan turned her head. Was that a faint knock on the courtyard slider or had she imagined it?

"Did you hear something?" Tom asked as he flicked a light switch and the courtyard grew bright.

A drab Hector absent his rainbow clothing stood at the door. Regan ran for a robe as Tom opened the slider.

"Forgive me for disturbing you. Can I come in? The

Practitioner has said prayers which I'm sure have helped, but it will take many more. Until he does his work, I don't like being outside after dark so close to your house."

"Yes, of course. Come in." Tom smiled obsequiously, still acting like he was Hector's friend and ally, but Regan had told him about the intimate conversation Hector had with the green-haired man so he was circumspect, too.

Regan returned, knotting the sash of her robe around her waist. "Do you want a cup of coffee? Something stronger?" she asked.

"No, thank you." Hector was willing to look at Tom, but he averted his eyes from her.

"Would you like to sit down in the living room?" Tom motioned Hector forward.

"No, thank you. I won't stay long; being here even for a short time is dangerous for me. I bring an offer and a plea for you to accept it. I've been contacted again by someone in the business — a local person, someone safe. I thought I would need to work to reestablish that connection, but everything has changed within the past couple of days."

Hector dropped his voice like someone might be listening as he spoke. "The FBI was on your new land a couple of nights ago. People were arrested. Of course, they didn't get the higher ups — they never do — so the woman is still in charge.

"You must agree to the proposal I bring you because we will all make a lot of money, and you, of all of us, have the most need to raise money. The Practitioner and the group have said prayers for your cat. What they've done may be enough to save him, however, the Practitioner doesn't know because he has never led prayers for a possessed animal before …" Hector sputtered to a pause and shrugged.

"But you must raise money to pay for other prayers, spirit prayers. It will be expensive because now three spirits walk your land who need to move to the next plane. It will require many prayers before they all can pass."

"Three spirits?" Regan questioned.

"Yes, three: Your Uncle Harry who you said watches over you here at your house, Pablo, who died outside your house, and the little girl."

"The little girl?" Regan asked, "Do you mean Chloe?"

"Yes. She is right here, too. I've seen her."

"You've seen her? Here?" Tom emphasized Hector's choice of location, "Here, on our land?"

Hector squirmed and avoided answering. "I thought once her father joined her, he would guide her spirit, but she doesn't go. She needs prayers to move on because even with her father's help she doesn't know how. She is a child, and as I have seen with my own eyes, children can be cruel in the way they think only of themselves. Being caught here as she is makes her dangerous.

"I am begging you. Please do what you need to do. Raise the money the Practitioner requires for his Prayers."

Tom looked at Regan, and with an expression couples share after some years together, wordlessly sought her opinion. She nodded.

"OK, Hector. We're in. How do we proceed?"

Hector's disposition brightened immediately. "Thank you. Thank you so much. I'll be in touch in a day or two."

As soon as Hector's taillights cleared the driveway, Tom

grabbed his wife and hugged her.

"I get it now, why you keep getting involved in your murder-solving exploits. It's exciting. Here we are poised to put an end to drug trafficking in our neighborhood. Why, we may be the ones to catch 'the woman'." Tom tried to sound like he was in a noir movie. "So what do you think, doll, should we drop a dime and tell Dave we're ready to send the dope peddlers to the big house?"

"Not tonight, Mr. Cagney. We have time before the Highly Sensitive Person known as Hector gets back to us." Regan began laughing, "I'm so tired right now that everything seems funny to me, especially Hector who sees the spirits of dead people, even ones like your uncle who doesn't exist. He must be an Extra Highly Sensitive Person to do that."

Tom's chuckle was followed by a yawn. "If I don't get some food and sleep soon, I'm going to be seeing spirits, too, so I've made two executive decisions. The first is pizza and the second is an early bedtime."

🏠🏠🏠🏠🏠🏠🏠🏠🏠🏠🏠

After a full undisturbed night's sleep, Hector's visions didn't seem so entertaining to Regan and trapping a drug lord didn't seem like such an appealing adventure to have.

She wanted to know if Tom had changed his mind, too, in the light of day, but he'd rushed out early for the monthly broker breakfast at 7:00 a.m., and when she tried to bring up Hector before he left, he had given her a quick peck and said,

"Later, sweetheart, I'm running late. We can talk at the office."

She'd been remiss because of distractions, but the personal life of a realtor was never an excuse for abandoning the fiduciary duty owed clients, so she was willing to put in a long morning's worth of work contacting contractors, escrow officers, and lenders, and in all ways monitoring her clients' buying and selling needs even if she regretted coming into the office to do it.

In the early morning her nose was assailed by the smell of scorched drywall and wooden framing, and the lingering fumes from roasted upholstery made her head hurt.

By late morning the contractors sent by their insurance company were on scene. They parked a huge dumpster in the driveway where the fire engine had been and began loud demolition work in her office. Power saws yowled, and when they paused, yelled instructions from workman to workman and chunks of debris being tossed into the dumpster kept the noise level consistently high.

Trying to work in the tiny storage room hastily designated as her makeshift office didn't help, either. She was a boss, however, and as such she was determined to set a good example by toughing it out even though all but one of their agents opted to work from home. She was there, she patted herself on the back, for the sake of that agent, and for Amanda who did her receptionist work valiantly if not without an occasional dramatic sniffle about the dreadfulness of her work environment.

It was into her miserable surroundings that Dave stumbled, having encountered first the bulky six-outlet electrical dock positioned just inside the doorway so she could power her phone, laptop, and a lamp from a plug-in down the hall and then the cable connecting her temporary landline to a phone jack by the reception desk.

His good eye squinted, forcing his prosthetic eye to follow suit. "What the heck are you thinking?" he bellowed.

"What do you mean?"

"Tom called and said you two are planning to set yourselves up as undercover agents, that's what I mean."

"If Tom called to tell you, why are you asking me what *I'm* thinking?"

"Because it's always you who gets into messes."

"Well, this time, it's both of us who are getting into a mess." She closed her eyes for an extended blink, "That didn't come out right, but you know what I mean."

Dave responded with a harrumph. "You and Tom are invited to my office after work tonight. Command performance. I want to get you to give up your crazy ideas, but if I can't, there's someone who'll be there who wants to explain a few things to you two. See you at 7:30."

Dave did the introductions. "Regan, Tom, this is Special Agent Rick Gibbons. He's the Field Officer out of the Palo Alto FBI office who's in charge of FBI operations here."

Special Agent Gibbons stood as Dave spoke. "So you're the people Officer Everett tells me have been approached by Hector Gonzales about some illicit operations, are you?"

"We are." Tom shook the hand Special Agent Gibbons extended.

Regan assessed him as she waited her turn to shake his hand. Perhaps she had seen too many TV shows featuring fit lantern-jawed FBI agents and set her expectations too high, but Special Agent Gibbons didn't match her ideal for a managing member of such an elite organization in any way. His dark hair was cut haphazardly and slicked down with old-style goo which made his two-day-shadow beard — a fashionable look she liked on most men — seem like a lack of good grooming. Worst of all, he had a paunch, not a small one that might have made jacket buttoning a bit stressful, but a large one which kept his jacket widely agape over it and forced him to balance with his feet turned out like a heavily pregnant woman. Or a duck.

His was an agenda handshake; he gripped her hand so hard it hurt. Trusting that he had established his superiority he quipped jovially, "So you're the little amateur sleuth Officer Everett told me about."

It would have been impolite to say she didn't appreciate his description of her so she smiled half-heartedly and said, "That would be me," and directed a glare at Dave.

"Officer Everett tells me he's not too happy about you getting involved in this operation. Ahh," he waved his hand, "we make use of the public in little ways all the time. I'm not worried about you. We cleaned up a nest of Colombians last week, knocked down their operation for the time being. We didn't get the higher-ups, not yet and they'll be back — they always come back — that's the nature of this beast. What we want to do is get some reliable people in place to let us know when they do. We need some fresh faces … like you two.

"We had someone on the inside; we rousted one Hector Gonzalez and have been using him as an unwilling informant, but we've gone about as far as we can with him. Now don't get me wrong, Hector's an opportunistic little operator who's been useful in the past. He's given us some OK information in exchange for us looking the other way about his gardening, but what he's been telling us lately hasn't been all that valuable."

Special Agent Gibbons snickered, "I guess to you untrained types that would look like Hector's buying immunity from prosecution, but sometimes you cut loose small fish to get the bigger ones. You know what I mean? Truth is we don't care about local growers or the people who use their product, not if you Californians want to look the other way when Federal laws get ignored.

"So we'll let you locals," he made it a point to direct his comment at Dave, "chase some little pot growers if you want. Or not; no skin off my nose."

Regan watched Dave as Special Agent Gibbons rolled on. Dave's jaw was clenched tightly.

"What we do worry about are smugglers who are bringing in cocaine and heroin and shipping it to the Midwest where there's a big problem with nice little ordinary people using it."

"These bigger fish that you mention," Tom asked, "is a man who goes by the name of Practitioner Fitzwater one of them?"

"Fitzwater? No, he's not any kind of fish, big or small. He's some guru Gonzalez likes, a former Christian Science leader who splintered off and formed his own winky quasi-religion. Why do you want to know about him?"

"Hector approached us because we said we needed the Practitioner's help. We wondered if Practitioner Fitzwater was part of the drug ring, but you're saying that involving us was all Hector's idea and that Fitzwater wasn't directing him?"

"That's right. Hector's a true believer. He thinks for a price that guy can lead a prayer group and perform miracles. Hector may use the Practitioner's services as a hook to get some prime growing real estate, but Fitzwater's not telling him to do it."

"I understand from," Regan was still reluctant to mention Melody, "a friend that Hector approached our dead neighbor, Paul Valentine, like he did us, with promises of help from the Practitioner when Paul's daughter was ill."

"Pablo Valentino," Regan was startled when Special Agent Gibbons used Paul's real name, "and Hector go way back. He kept in touch with his hometown friend — casually — but when he heard his old friend owned acreage — I told you Hector was opportunistic — he got in touch, thinking he could talk his friend into growing cannabis.

"When he heard about Valentino's kid being deathly ill, he knew he had the perfect win-win: he could get prayers for Valentino's daughter — which he believed would save her life — and at the same time set up a nice profitable little business for himself."

"Hector said he had a connection — that's what he told us," Tom said, "someone in the business who could help with selling what we grew ..."

Special Agent Gibbons cut Tom off with another hand wave, "Guys like Hector always know someone who knows someone who knows someone; the pot growing community is one big happy family. We don't care about them; they're for the likes of the Santa Cruz Police Department and the County Sherriff, oh, and Officer Everett. Like I said before, we're after the guys who smuggle."

Regan noted Dave's expression was as blank and unmoving as it would have been had his artificial eye controlled his sighted eye instead of the other way around.

"The big fish," Tom asked, "what makes you think they'll come back through us?"

"History. That's what they did last time. After Hector got Pablo and his wife on board, someone got greedy and kicked the operation up a notch from pot growing to drug smuggling, too. It could have been Hector or Pablo, although my gut says no," he shrugged, "or the connection. Or even more likely, the woman said to be running the whole show."

"Melody," Dave stated.

"Possibly," Special Agent Gibbons equivocated. "There's no denying the operation took off after her husband came on board, but she has no drug background — no criminal background at all — so she may have been nothing more than the poor dumb little wife. I wouldn't call making her the mystery woman a slam-dunk. Not at all.

"Now Hector wouldn't agree with me. He thinks she's the one we're after, but he's biased. Hey, you're going to be spending time with him, I'm sure he'll tell you all about it," Special Agent Gibbons laughed. "Me, I don't buy much of what Hector says. My opinion of Hector? He fits in perfectly in Santa Cruz; he's as big a winky as Fitzwater is."

As Special Agent Gibbons rolled on, Regan regretted having glared at Dave earlier. The man was a blowhard who went out of his way to belittle Dave and his associates every time he could. She hoped Dave would recognize she sided with him by the way she phrased her question for Special Agent Gibbons.

"I know we'll never be able to rise to your level of expertise, but what is it you want us amateurs to do to help you?"

"Simple. Play along with Hector. Don't worry about committing any crimes; local authorities will get lucky and intercept your product just as it's ready to be harvested. What you're going to be looking for is those bigger fish. If you get any insight as to who's in charge, you let me know. If it looks like a cartel is getting friendly again, you let me know."

"See, guys," Dave spoke to Regan and Tom, "that's the part I don't like ..."

A third interrupting hand wave materialized. "Fine, let Officer Everett know over dinner, if that's the way you want to work it. He can bring me in."

He addressed the rest of his instructions to Dave. "Just make sure you call me, not the Homeland Security people. The FBI does all the leg work while they put out the cute little phrases like, 'If you see something, say something' and get all the funding. I want to catch these sharks and not let them take the credit for it."

It had only been a week since the fire, but the sheetrock was up, taped, textured, and painted in Regan's repaired office and the roof was intact overhead. Her broken window was replaced with one matching the rest of the office windows.

She had a "new" desk and office chair purchased from nearby Restore, the Habitat for Humanity retail store where donated goods were sold cheaply and the proceeds used to build homes for low-income families. The desk worked surprisingly well and Regan was beginning to think she'd miss it when she donated it again after the real replacement desk she ordered arrived. She didn't feel the same wistfulness about her temporary office chair, however.

"Can I close your door, Regan?" Burt, one of their agents, said as he poked his head into her redone space. "The whole office smells of paint and it's making me sneeze." He demonstrated the paint effect with a loud "Hah-guzzu!"

"Sure, go ahead."

She sniffed the air after he enclosed her. *I like the smell of fresh paint.*

"Regan, Ms. Buchanan is here to see you and she's bearing gifts." Amanda's voice was upbeat over the newly installed office intercom.

"Send her down."

Regan reopened her office door — so much for her sensitive associate's allergies — so a beaming Melody and the four men following in her wake, struggling with two huge paper-covered parcels, could come inside.

"If yeu deuna' like them, I'll take them back, but when I saw them — they're covered in Clan Buchanan plaid — I had to get them. I remember sittin' in the wingback chairs you lost in the fire and havin' tea; I want us teu deu that again. I see once and future business between us, so these are my gift teu yeu after what yeu've been through because of me."

Melody ripped at the paper of one of the parcels before the workmen finished up-righting it and placing it on the floor. "It's an ancient tartan color so it's muted, but it still has a rainbow of colors — blues, greens, marigold, mauve, and a couple shades of soft orange — so yeu have many options for decoratin' around it. What deu yeu think?"

Regan might have lied to Melody if she didn't care for the chairs because Melody was so excited with her gifts. But Regan didn't have to. She loved them.

"Wow. They're perfect. Thank you so much," she said as she gave Melody a hug. "Shall we get some tea and christen them?"

"I canna' today. I have an appointment," Melody looked at her watch, "in about four minutes," she laughed, "so I have teu run."

"Thanks again," Regan called after the hastily departing

Melody and then she closed her door again in deference to her sensitively-nosed colleague.

Tom came into her office about two hours after Melody left to find Regan sitting with her chin on her hands staring at her gifts. He glanced at his wife, looked at where she was staring hard, and then returned his attention to Regan.

"What's up? You don't look happy," he frowned.

"It's the chairs, well the chairs and some other things I've been thinking about; they're giving me a headache."

"The chairs? Are you sure it's not the paint fumes that are bothering you? The smell is overwhelming in here. Open your door. Shall I open the window, too?"

"I tried. It must be installed incorrectly. It doesn't open."

Tom gave it a try before acknowledging she was right. "I'll talk to the contractor."

He pushed the door to her office open as wide as it would go and fanned it back and forth before he pressed it fully open against one of her walls.

He sat down and wiggled a bit in one of the chairs. "I like the pattern. The feel is too upright for me, but not bad. Are these more Restore finds?"

"Melody brought them. They're her clan's plaid. They're a gift to replace the chairs the fire destroyed."

"That was nice of her ..."

"Did you tell her about the fire when you talked to her on the 17th?"

Tom thought for a moment. "It never came up."

"Then how did she know I needed new chairs? Our fire never made the local TV news because the night's stories were all about people filing last-minute tax returns. We did get a brief mention in the *Santa Cruz Sentinel*, but it was a three-inch story below the fold on page five, hardly something Melody would have noticed even if for some strange reason she subscribed to our local paper.

"I've been thinking; Melody knows my car. She saw it when I went to her house. She said she was on her way to our house on the 17th, but stopped because she saw my car parked outside our new property. Tom, she knows what I drive."

"And?"

"She would have recognized my car parked out back the night of the fire. She's been in my office, too, and knows where it is in the office scheme. We assumed she was at home with her injured James, but suppose she wasn't? Melody could have been our fire-bomber."

"Ahh, Regan," he shook his head half-heartedly.

"Tom, maybe it was Hector who threw the firebomb on her order. Maybe it's the rainbow of colors on the chairs that started me wondering, but they reminded me of Hector, the Practitioner's rainbow-clothed man. Melody talked to him at Chloe's party. I saw her. I remember Hector took her hand in both of his. At the time I thought it was a gesture of goodwill, but suppose it was a gesture of deference?"

"Deference?"

"Yes, deference, like kissing the Godfather's ring." Regan looked uneasy. "Remember I thought Hector was the hit-and-run driver who crashed into Melody and James? I thought he did it because of animosity. Dave agrees with me that Hector probably was the one who hit Melody and James, but he gives Hector a different motive.

"He thinks the accident was staged and that Melody ordered the hit. Dave thinks Hector was never trying to hurt Melody; he was just making her look like a victim. He thinks that's why a truck taking on James's car didn't hurt either of them seriously.

"Maybe Melody knew I needed new chairs because Hector told her the firebombing she ordered was a success and my office and everything in it was destroyed." Regan became more and more agitated as she spoke. "Melody said something when she dropped off the chairs that's been bothering me."

"What was that?"

"She said we had done business in the past and she looked forward to us doing business in the future. Tom, do you think I've been wrong about her? Do you think Dave's right? Do you think she's 'the woman' everyone's trying to identify?"

Tom motioned for her to come to him and patted the other Clan Buchanan chair. When she sat down, he leaned toward her and took her hands in his. "I see what a strain the last couple of weeks have been on you. I see you stringing together a series of events that may or may not be connected. You've been so certain about Melody, about her innocence in all of this. Are you sure you should change your mind based on a series of flimsy coincidences? It doesn't seem like you."

"I'm not sure of anything anymore. That's the problem."

"Couldn't Melody have heard about the fire, innocently, from Hector when you saw them talking, and being a generous person and grateful for your support, she decided to give you a gift ..."

"Believe me, I thought of that. If Hector talked to Melody

about the fire, was it because he knew about it since he caused it? He has no motive unless Melody sent him to do the dirty work."

"He has no motive unless *someone* sent him; it doesn't have to have been Melody."

A smile momentarily lit up Regan's face. "You're right," but it was short lived, fading as quickly as it appeared. "Who, though?"

Regan's mouth opened wordlessly as she recalled a memory. "You know," she answered her own question, "Hector could have heard about our fire from the green-haired man. They were talking at the party for Chloe. And, of course he knew about our fire because he and Taylor were there right after it started."

Regan sneered, "Unless I'm right about that nasty little woman and her green-haired toady and they started it. Everyone thinks so highly of Taylor Bingham because of her environmental stance. I seem to be her only detractor — well, Melody agrees, she sees the same unpleasantness in her that I do."

Tom made an effort to sound positive. "So, you and Melody are on the same side about Taylor Bingham. Does that mean you're ready to rethink your rethink about her?"

"Maybe," Regan said tentatively. "It does seem there may be ways she could have heard about the fire without being the one who did it or the one who ordered it," but Regan was still full of uncertainty.

"I'm going to tackle the question head-on. When I call her to say thanks again for the chairs, I'm going to ask her straight out how she found out about our fire. Hopefully I'll catch her off guard and whatever answer she gives will be the truth." Regan wagged her head. "I sure hope she has a good answer."

"You take on Melody, I'll handle Hector. We have a meeting later today."

"When do we see him?"

"Just me for the meeting; he was clear about today being males only." Tom grinned, "What can I say, sweetheart, I'm the one he likes best. I'll sound him out about if and how he knew about our fire and if he told Melody." Tom wrinkled his nose. "It's only reasonable for me to know what he knows and how he gets his information now that we're business partners."

By the time Tom came home Regan had a good start on dinner and felt better about Melody's virtue. Granted she would have preferred being face to face with Melody and reading her eyes and her body language instead of asking over the phone, but Melody had answered so perfunctorily that she was either telling the truth or she had a convincing answer ready to use for a question she shouldn't have been expecting. Regan gladly chose to believe her answer was honest.

When Regan asked how she knew about the office fire, Melody answered simply: "Hector told me."

Regan had followed up with, "You and Hector are on speaking terms?" She hadn't mentioned the conversation she saw them having on the 17th.

"We are now. Warily. He says he feels better about me now that Paul has forgiven him."

"Hector says he's talked to Paul?" The confusion Regan felt was clear in her tone of voice.

"Oh, no, Regan, Paul hasn't been talkin' teu him; he says Chloe has."

"He told you your daughter ..."

"Yes. My daughter; he says *my* daughter speaks teu *him*. I canna say whether he's just crazy or if he's one of the most insensitive people I've ever met."

Regan did a core dump of the conversation she'd had with Melody on Tom before he'd finished docking his cell phone. "That explains the stiffness I saw in Melody when I saw her talking to Hector."

"The Highly Sensitive Person Hector not only sees the presence of spirits that don't exist, he talks to dead people, too. I'm awed," Tom said flippantly. "He has some impressive abilities."

"Did you ask him how he knew about our office fire? Did he envision it or have a hand in it?"

"He says neither of those ways. He said a friend of his told him about it."

"Who was it?"

"I pressed; he said he forgot. Sorry," Tom apologized. "I may not have gotten any useful information out of him about his source, but I did discover he likes contracts that formally detail criminal arrangements."

"What do you mean?"

"You're going to see. He wants to meet with you tomorrow. You're to rendezvous at the third brussels sprouts field past the Dimeo Road dump at high noon," Tom said gravely.

"Where?"

He started to laugh. "He'll be parked in the Davenport Roadhouse parking lot at the back near the old jail. He drives a beat-up old green Chevy sedan; you'll spot him easily. My guess is that he'll have you follow him to one of the coastal fields up Highway 1. He does seem to like being surrounded by brussels sprouts for all his illicit business. That's where he took me when he approached me about growing and that's where we went today for our big contract signing."

🏠🏠🏠🏠🏠🏠🏠🏠🏠🏠🏠🏠

Tom was right, Hector's car was easy to spot. The Davenport Roadhouse was an upscale restaurant and Hector's old Chevy Lumina was atypical among the lunch-goer's vehicles parked in the lot.

The jail was a designated Historic Building officially called the Historic Jail. The one-cell prison was used only twice since it was built in the early 1900s and is a museum now, but closed during weekdays until the summer tourist season hits full swing. She had no difficulty finding a parking place next to Hector's car.

He motioned to her to put down her window. His passenger side window was already down and he called out to her through their adjacent open windows, "Get in, Regan."

She complied, but it took a second attempt at closing the tinny-sounding door before it latched. Hector began backing up immediately.

"Where are we going?" Regan made sure her voice held a hint of concern as they pulled on to Highway 1 and headed north in the direction of San Francisco.

"Not far. We can have some privacy up the road."

As Tom promised, Hector turned toward a brussels sprouts

field on an unpaved farmer's road. He stopped once they had driven over a slight mound which made them, if not completely hidden from the Highway, somewhat out of sight. It occurred to Regan that, given Hector's car, any passing traffic would assume it belonged to a field worker.

Hector didn't look directly at her as he fidgeted and pressed his lips together. "I should search you, you know, make sure you aren't recording what I say, but I trust you, I think."

"It's just us," she reassured him, glad that his discomfort and embarrassment meant she wouldn't have to endure a pat-down.

He reached across her and opened his glove box. "I have a paper for you to sign," he said as he pulled out a crisp typed page and a pen and handed them to her.

There wasn't much on it; Regan read it over quickly. The document was dated and outlined a brief contract between her and an unnamed entity agreeing that, for a fifty-percent share of future marijuana growing profits, she made her property available for the production, processing, and distribution of recreational cannabis.

"Only marijuana? Nothing else like heroin poppies, cocaine, or methamphetamines?"

"No. I only know how to grow marijuana on land like yours and meth is bad stuff. It can blow up."

"I see my name on here, but I don't see anyone else's name. Who am I agreeing to let use my land?"

"Don't worry about who. Just sign the agreement and let's go."

"I deal with contracts every day. It's not a legally binding document unless it's signed by both parties to the agreement." She returned the paper to him and bluffed, hoping her realtor-related understanding of contracts might throw him off balance enough he would name names.

Her ploy didn't work. He thrust the paper back at her. "Someone has to go first. You sign it and then my connection will sign it."

She crossed her arms and pondered how hard she should try pushing him.

"Please don't make a problem," he implored. "I've already been given an advance which I've given to Practitioner Fitzwater. Your cat should be well by now for sure."

Regan thought she saw an opening and took a chance. "And I gather after payment to the Practitioner that Chloe has stopped worrying you, too."

Hector's whole body tensed. He looked directly at her for the first time. "Yes." His breathing was audible. "How did you know?"

She smiled as enigmatically as the Mona Lisa. "I'm a lot like you are. Spirits sometimes speak to me, too."

"Are you a Highly Sensitive Person, too?" he asked guilelessly.

Her intention had been to discombobulate Hector so she could take control of the conversation. Now she saw another opening; she tried flattery and empathy.

"No, Hector, I'm not. Sometimes I feel things, but it's not the same. I've been given information, but not in the way you are. There are very few people like you. You're special. You hear other-worldly voices while the spirits who speak to me do so only through intuition and careful observation, that's all.

"I've heard you hint. I know you need to talk to someone who understands. Have you told anyone the full story?"

"I've told no one, not even the Practitioner. He's such a great man, but even he ..."

"I understand, Hector. His skills lie elsewhere. You want to unburden yourself to someone who can understand. Someone like me."

He lapsed into his native Spanish, vulnerable in front of her. "Si, Señora."

"When did Chloe speak to you? What did she say?"

Hector was silent for so long that Regan feared she had over-played her hand.

"The first time was in your backyard when Pablo killed himself."

It was her turn to gasp. "You were the one there with him?"

"I was the one he was chasing."

"Paul — Pablo — was trying to kill you?"

"No," Hector sounded aggrieved. "He wouldn't have harmed me. He didn't harm me. He was a good shot. If he wanted to shoot me, he wouldn't have missed. When I stopped running, he stopped shooting. If he wanted to kill me, he could have then."

Regan rephrased her question. "Why was he chasing you?"

"He was mad at me. He blamed me for so much."

"Did he blame you for Chloe, for her death?"

"For that he blamed himself. But when he stopped shooting, I reminded him of his guilt. I shouted at him that if he hadn't waited when I came to him with my plan, she could have been saved. I should never have said that even if it was true."

"Then tell me, what did he blame you for?"

"He thought I was trying to steal from him that night, that's why he was so mad. I wasn't, though. I didn't go to his house to steal from him. After Chloe died, Pablo said Melody wanted him to stop working with me and quit the business. Pablo told me he agreed to do that, but then I found out he hadn't quit.

"Rumors started about the business being run by a man and a woman. I thought my friend lied to me, that she made him lie to me. I thought Pablo and Melody forced me out and kept my connection for themselves. That's what my connection told me they did. He said Pablo and Melody were getting rich, too, without me.

"I've been a little down on my luck so my connection said I should ask Pablo to give me some money since he could afford to. After taking over and pushing me out, that's the least he could do. So I was going to ask for some money and remind him how betrayed I felt; that's the reason I went to his house that night.

"He wasn't home when I got there, and I admit, I forced his lock and let myself in. I sat in his house and waited for him to come home, but I kept getting madder and madder when I thought about Melody and him getting rich with my connection, so I decided I better leave before I lost control of myself."

Hector was downcast as he went on. "I admit, too, that before I left, I decided to take a little reward for all my hard work, without asking. I was looking through the dresser in his bedroom, looking for money — not to steal it, just to borrow some — when he came home.

"He found me there and started screaming that I was looking for his evidence, that she had sent me to steal it. He got his gun and I started running and he started chasing me."

"What kind of evidence did he think you were sent to steal?"

"The evidence he had on the woman running things. What he said made no sense to me, because Melody was the woman running the operation with him.

"When he caught up to me, I started yelling about how he betrayed me. He yelled back that he loved Melody so much that's what he had to do."

*Those were the unintelligible words that Regan and Tom heard.*

"That's when the child came. She was there suddenly in a cloud of light, shining in the darkness. She called Pablo daddy and said she was so lonely. She started to cry and said she was lost and that she needed him to come to her and help her find her way. Then she said if he wouldn't come, she would find her mother and take her instead.

"Pablo was in agony. He screamed in pain. And then he put the gun in his mouth and went to her."

Regan could feel her heart pounding as she remembered the barely human sound she'd heard before the last gunshot. She had heard Paul's final anguish as he had to make a choice: live and risk Melody's life, or die and be with his daughter.

"The child, what happened to her?"

"I don't know. I ran away."

"And now you've seen her again?"

"No, not seen her, only heard her. She has come to me as I sleep."

"You had a dream about her?"

"It wasn't a dream. I was in bed, but awake — I know I was awake because the first time she spoke I ran out of my room to get away from her. She said Paul was angry at me, he and the child were angry because Practitioner Fitzwater wasn't helping them and it was my fault for not raising money for his prayer group. The child told me I must get help for them or she and Pablo would seek revenge against me."

"So, you came to us," Regan said.

"You see why I had to?"

"I do, Hector." Regan's sympathy was genuine.

"I told my connection you and your husband had agreed to work with me and he gave me an advance of money which I gave to the Practitioner. His group is already praying and on Saturday night, right before the celebration, I heard the child's voice again.

"This time she was happy and she said Paul had forgiven me for my crime. The prayers had worked. They were going to the next plane.

"But you see why you must sign?" Hector's agitation grew once more. "If you don't, my connection will want his money back and I don't have it to give him. He will kill me."

Regan scribbled her signature on Hector's paper. "We wouldn't want that."

"Thank you." He took her hand in both of his like Regan had seen him do with Melody. *Gratitude, not deference,* she thought.

"Hector, who is your connection?"

She could read his hesitation; he wanted to tell her. But his longing vanished quickly and was replaced by fear. "I cannot say. Please understand if I tell you, he will kill me. I'm sure of it."

Regan and Tom clipped on the visitor badges that Dave left for them at the front desk of the Santa Cruz Police Department and waited as the duty officer buzzed to unlock the security door. Once past the entry room they took the stairs at the back of the building to the second floor and walked to Dave's office.

"Regan, you brought Tom with you so this must be some serious info you're going to drop on me," he teased by way of greeting them. "What wild surmises do you have for me this time?"

"No surmises, Dave," Tom spoke for them.

"Just facts," Regan added.

"OK then," he did his best imitation of Dragnet's Sergeant Joe Friday, "just the facts, ma'am."

"Paul Valentine was murdered."

"That dead horse again," Dave said, clearly disappointed.

"Technically he committed suicide, but he was driven to it by another party. There was a witness," Tom said.

Dave rocked forward on his seat as he spoke. "An eyeball witness, not just an ear witness like you two?"

"An eyeball witness," Regan said trying hard to sound calm. "We know who Paul Valentine was chasing. He witnessed what we heard. He's the one who told us what happened."

"Yes?" Dave gave them a give-it-to me wave of his hand.

"It was Hector Gonzalez," Regan proclaimed, no longer able to control her excitement.

Dave rocked back in his chair. "Practitioner Fitzwater's rainbow-man and known giver of information the FBI says is no longer reliable? Wow, what a news flash. If you want, I'll get a hold of Special Agent Gibbons 'cause this sounds too big-time for me to handle." He let his sarcasm land fully. "And here I thought you were serious."

Regan replied with such fervor her voice went up an octave. "We are serious. Hector said Chloe Valentine's ghost appeared and told Paul she needed a parent and wanted him to join her. She said if he wouldn't, she'd take her mother, Melody, instead."

Dave started to laugh. "This gets better and better. I've never heard of a 'the ghost made me do it' murder before."

"Of course it wasn't a ghost, Dave." Regan sighed dramatically. "It was a third person pretending to be the ghost of Chloe Valentine."

Dave tilted his head back and drawled, "Ooohh."

"But the fact that the ghost impersonator said what it did, well, that makes Paul's suicide a murder, doesn't it? The ghost gave him no choice; he had to kill himself to protect his wife."

"I don't know. A soon-to-be-divorced man like him; you'd think he would tell the ghost to go ahead and take the little woman," Dave snickered.

"Not if he still loved her!" Regan was as exasperated with Dave's reply as she had ever been with any of his quips. "Not if he felt responsible for" — she almost blurted out 'making her a criminal,' but she stopped before she said it — "not if he felt guilty about all sorts of things in their past."

"Ghosts aside, Dave, it seems there was a third person present on our hillside when Paul Valentine took his life," Tom reasoned, "and that person was a contributing factor in what happened.

"Now I know you might think that Hector — or anyone involved with Practitioner Fitzwater's tribe — might not make the most reliable witness, especially when they talk about spirits and ghosts, but his story about what happened fills in a lot of blanks and is consistent with what we heard."

"I'll be sure to let Special Agent Gibbons know about this — discovery — you two made so he can ask Mr. Gonzales all about it next time he chats with him about his drug dealings," Dave said. "The chat's gonna' be soon, too. Did I forget to mention there's just been an arrest warrant issued for your ghost-seeing pal? My bad.

"Yep. After a number of days of questioning, the FBI thinks they finally got a break from one of the guys busted last week on your new property. The perp called the local drug connection 'El Arco Iris,' which, if my Spanish is any good, is the rainbow man.

"It took Gibbons a few days to figure out what he meant, but in the end Special Agent Gibbons thinks he did. It was kind of a surprise to everyone, but it seems your rainbow-wearing Hector is something of an Academy Award winning actor, playing the role of little informant to us and feeding real but not very important info to the FBI while running the show with 'the woman."

"Anyway, Special Agent Gibbons is on to him now and says he looks good to be elevated from minor pot grower, not of any interest to the Feds, to the male ringleader who plays nice with the major drug smuggler and is of great interest to them."

Regan was incredulous. "That can't be right, Dave. Melody says neither Paul nor Hector would get involved with Colombians, that they left their homeland because of just those sorts."

"Melody told you that?" The still recumbent Dave splayed his hands across his middle.

"Yes."

"Would this be the same Melody so many of us in law enforcement like as the female head of the operation?" He smiled as broadly as the Cheshire Cat. "Well then, it must be true."

At work the next day, Regan was still brooding about Melody and Hector as she sat on her uncomfortable Restore chair and cast an occasional glance at the beautiful plaid wingchairs Melody had given her.

Dave thought it was only a matter of time before Hector gave up his female partner and said he expected the name to be Melody Buchanan. Regan protested in front of him, but alone with Tom she confessed to once again sharing the same thought.

The only piece that didn't fit was Hector's final statement that, if he told Regan the name of his connection, the man would kill him. *His words sounded sincere, but then, if he was that good at playing us all along …*

She was dragged from her thoughts by Amanda trying to sound positive and cheery as she spoke over the office intercom.

"Regan, are you in your office? I haven't seen you yet today so you may not be. If you are, Taylor Bingham and her friend … Pardon me, ma'am? … and her associate, Christopher Smith, are here to see you. If you don't answer, I guess it's because you aren't in your office."

*Oh good grief, the last people in the world I want to see are Taylor and the green-haired man.* Regan remained silent. *Note to self, considering the way Amanda is trying to offer me cover, I must talk to Tom about giving her a raise.*

A happy-faced pixie poked her head into Regan's office. "Good morning, Regan. I thought it was worth checking on you in case the intercom wasn't working properly and you didn't hear your receptionist say we were here to see you."

Regan didn't even attempt to smile or be welcoming as Taylor and a changed Christopher invaded her office and arranged themselves on Melody's wingchairs. She didn't register Taylor's droning about how well her office was coming back together because she could only focus on Christopher.

His long grassy hair was gone, replaced by a cropped and styled sprouting of brown hair. He looked entirely normal and civilized and his demeanor matched his look. Even the gash above his eyebrow was under control, Regan thought, by the careful administration of some makeup.

"Yes, Taylor, Mrs. McHenry's office is looking very nice," he said, personifying the definition of obsequious.

Regan couldn't help it; she blurted out, "Christopher, what's happened to your hair?"

He and Taylor fairly twittered, filling the room with enthralled laughter.

"I got tired of it. I change my hair color all the time to keep it interesting."

"And here I thought your green hair was a statement about your environmental sympathies."

"Well, it was, sort of," Taylor broke in. "But now Christopher wants to make a new statement. He wants you to know that as your new tenant, he will be a quiet middle-of-the-road person who will no longer call attention to himself. You can see that just by looking at him, can't you? So now you have no reason not to rent to him, do you?"

"Taylor, the color of Christopher's hair has never been a problem with me. We won't be renting to him because I don't like him." Regan smiled spitefully and enjoyed doing so as she and Taylor spoke about Christopher like he wasn't in the room.

Taylor started their conversation with sunshine and light when she thought Regan could be manipulated to do what she wanted. The rancorous Taylor reemerged when their meeting didn't go as she planned.

"I'll give you a few days to talk things over with your husband; I'm sure you'll reconsider." Her words themselves weren't threatening, but their delivery was.

"Or what, Taylor? What will you and Christopher do? Start another protest? Throw another rock? Start another fire?"

"Come, Christopher." Taylor left as she had on other occasions: in a huff. But this time she was dragging a no-longer green-haired man with her.

Xerox copies of the agreement Hector had Tom and Regan sign appeared at their office the next day. They hadn't been mailed. Both arrived in the same sealed envelope and were put through the front door mail slot sometime after the office was closed for the night. Tom's name was typed on it so Amanda brought the envelope to him.

Tom called Dave and asked him to stop by, even before he mentioned the envelope and its contents to Regan. He had, though, by the time Dave walked down the hall on his way to Tom's office, poked his head into Regan's space, and summoned her with a tilt of his head and two words: "Come on."

She joined them as soon as she wrapped up her phone conversation with a seller client and discovered Dave was wearing latex gloves as he studied the contents of the envelope.

"There's not much to go on, but if you two weren't already part of the investigation and authorized to play along, I'd say these papers make you look guilty as hell."

"They aren't countersigned. Hector said the person we

were making the contract with would sign after we signed them," Regan said.

"And you believed him? Why would a drug lord admit they were a drug lord by signing a paper?" Dave asked. "These look like enforcement papers to me; something to let you know you better keep your part of the bargain."

Tom nodded his agreement. "Do you think Hector dropped them off?"

"He hasn't been picked up yet," Dave replied, "so he could have, but I'm not sure why he would. More likely these came from his partner who's just reminding you they exist and that they're in her possession."

Dave reached into one of the pockets on his Hawaiian shirt — today's version of his trademark apparel was predominantly yellow, green, and orange — and produced a folded plastic bag.

"Do you mind if I take these?" he asked as he unfurled the bag. "Couldn't hurt to run them for prints, see if we come up with any matches."

🏠🏠🏠🏠🏠🏠🏠🏠🏠🏠🏠

Tom answered their home phone when it rang that evening and listened intently with only a brief, "Interesting," a quick "Uh huh," and a "Thanks for letting me know; I'll tell Regan," breaking his silence.

"Tell me what?" Regan asked.

"That was Dave. They did tests on the envelope and papers and the only fingerprints they found were ours."

"You mean whoever sent the papers doesn't have prints on record?"

"No. There were no other prints on anything. Dave thinks whoever made the copies wore gloves like he did.

"There's more, sweetheart." Tom sat on the kitchen stool next to her and took her hand. "At about 10:00 this morning Taylor Bingham was out for one of her morning hikes and was taking a path that runs through our new property ... she found Hector's body."

Regan gasped like she had been hit in the solar plexus.

Regan went through the motions of working by holding a broker's open for her new listing, but neither her head nor her heart was in it. She missed opportunities to encourage agents to show the house and she failed to ask the sorts of questions that could prompt agents to think about their clients and consider which of them might be a good match for the house.

She felt guilty for imagining Hector died as a warning to her — she wasn't normally that self-centered — and yet she couldn't shake the thought that he had. She needed — needed badly — to talk to Dave and tell him why she hadn't slept the night before and who she suspected of killing Hector, even though he would laugh at her.

Her open house was in Aptos and was part of the afternoon broker tour. When the tour ended at 3:00, she drove to the Santa Cruz Police Department and asked the duty officer if Dave was in and free.

"No ma'am," the officer said as he scanned the officer-in-the-building log on the computer. "Officer Everett isn't in at the moment."

"Yes, he is," Dave's familiar voice rang out from behind her. "You can log me back in, Dan. The mayor's all filled in about how the Baker and Butler families are doing; she likes to keep tabs on them. Can you believe how long it's been since Butch and Elizabeth were killed in the line of duty? It seems like it was just a couple of months ago."

Dave stopped reminiscing with his fellow officer and took a real look at Regan; he saw a troubled friend. "You look awful. What's up?" he frowned. He grabbed a visitor's badge off the counter, "Come on up with me."

He ushered her into the break room and pointed to the coffee setup. "Let's grab some," he said. She could feel him watching her as she poured coffee into a cup and added more sugar than she normally did. She knew she was being assessed.

"Dave, about Hector...," Regan said as she sat opposite him in front of his desk.

"Yeah, I know. It's not like you two were pals, but you knew him and saw him just a couple of days before ... it makes what he did more personal. You couldn't have known he was gonna kill himself, though."

"What?" Regan breathed.

"Looks like he walked out into the woods and shot himself just like his buddy Paul did. The good thing from where you sit, it's getting real hard to make the case that your pal Melody was involved in Hector's death. It doesn't look like she killed him or ordered a hit on him to tidy up or to keep him from outing her, not since he died by his own hand."

Dave's mouth turned up at the corners almost imperceptibly. "Even Special Agent Gibbons says he's stuck because, if the woman everyone is so hot to catch isn't her; we're back to square one in the investigation.

"You sure are quiet, Regan. What did you want to see me about?" He tried to tease her in a friendly way to draw her out. "You got another of your wild notions? You want to talk killer ghosts again?"

"You may be closer to the truth than you think you are, Dave," Regan said softly.

She put her untouched coffee on his desk. "I want to check on a few things. I'll get back to you."

"Awh, come on, Regan. Tell me now. It's been a long day and I could use a good laugh."

She ignored him, already lost in her own thoughts.

He called after her as she left, "Just don't do anything stupid."

Regan's initial research was a safe venture; all that was involved was her computer and some patience. She had a hunch, but before telling Dave what it was, or asking Tom how far she should go with it, she wanted to prove to herself that the odds were high that she was right.

She sat at her computer and entered "Christopher Smith" and "photos." She got fifty-seven pages of hits. Christopher Smith, it turned out was an incredibly common name.

Since the two of them shared the same environmental interests, if she couldn't aim directly at Christopher, she might be able to find him through Taylor. She tried again using "Taylor Bingham" and "photos" as the keywords. Almost as many pages popped up under her name as for Christopher. Taylor was a highly photographed woman it seemed, too frequently a photographed subject to help with Regan's search.

She made a third attempt adding "Christopher Smith" to "Taylor Bingham photos" before hitting the search button. The numbers at the bottom of the screen indicated there were only three pages of photos where both of them had been tagged for her to study.

*That's doable.*

Her search proved quick and easy. She printed the photos that supported her theory and had enough to prove her point before she left the second page.

The next part of her research wasn't going to be any more dangerous and she hoped it would be as straightforward. It was also another test of her theory. According to Hector, their property already was home to three dead spirits. Uncle Harry might be made up, but the unearthly Paul and Chloe were more than enough spectral neighbors; she didn't want Hector joining them. At least that's what she planned to tell Practitioner Fitzwater when she asked for his help.

🏠🏠🏠🏠🏠🏠🏠🏠🏠🏠🏠

Tom wanted to come with her and she was glad to have his company. Practitioner Fitzwater agreed to see them on his terms, on his timeframe, and on their property. At the appointed meeting time they found an ancient big-finned

Cadillac parked near the entrance to Paul's land and figured it belonged to the Practitioner. When they had parked and walked a few yards onto the property, they spotted him with his back to them sitting cross-legged and Buddha-like near where he had conducted last Sunday's services. His head was bowed and he seemed altogether smaller than he had the last time they saw him. That changed as he raised his hands skyward and began speaking in an unrecognizable language like he had on the 17th. There was magic in his voice.

Tom and Regan held back, leaning together holding hands as they waited for him to finish his chant. It seemed the Practitioner had eyes in the back of his head; he didn't move or turn to see them, nevertheless he became aware of them and invited them to come join him.

They sat on the ground in front of him, Regan glad she had worn jeans. She clasped and unclasped her hands; the Practitioner and their story about Uncle Harry made her nervous.

Tom spoke first. "Uncle Harry is better; even his coat is improved. Your prayers have worked. Thank you. You don't need to do more for him."

*One spirit, the imaginary one, down.*

"You know about Hector, of course?" Regan asked.

"Of course. I was saying prayers for him because I fear he is troubled and will be unable to move forward."

"We are so sorry for your loss."

"We all leave this earth at some point." The Practitioner smiled in his benign way.

Regan shifted and pulled her knees under her chin. "I spoke with Hector the day before he took his life. He said

Chloe Valentine called her father to her before his suicide and that he had heard her voice as well. He was afraid of Chloe and afraid Paul and Chloe might ask him to come to them. If they did, would he have?"

"I sense guilt in you, guilt in both of you, that neither of you should carry." The Practitioner reached a hand toward Regan's knee and patted it kindly.

Tom confessed, "We encouraged Hector in something, Practitioner Fitzwater, and it may have been what cost him his life."

"Knowing Hector, what caused his death started well before you knew him. Hector didn't tell me what he did away from the group. He had a fondness for money — many of us do and are not careful about how we come by it — but he had a good heart, too. He would never tell me what he did for fear I would cast him out of our community. How ironic. I know he held me in high regard and yet thought I would be so petty."

Regan held her hand out to Tom who reached into his jacket and produced the folded printouts she had made.

"You did ask this man to leave, though, didn't you?" she said as she handed them to the Practitioner.

He looked through them slowly, pausing after each one. "Yes. His heart was not kind. This young man had such promise and such brutality in him."

"Christopher and Hector, were they friends?" Regan asked.

"Hector joined us shortly before I asked Christopher to leave. I wouldn't say they were close, but they knew one another through the community. I never explained to the

Prayers why Christopher was dismissed. I wonder now, if Hector saw what I did to Christopher and feared I would do the same to him? I never explained Christopher's dismissal; I should have, but I wanted to spare Christopher's reputation and I assumed a Highly Sensitive Person like Hector would figure it out. In retrospect I regret my decision. I may have inadvertently frightened Hector. Perhaps I'm the one who should feel guilty about him."

The Practitioner raised his hand skyward once more. "Paul and now Hector remain here. We will pray for them to find their way to the next plane, but not from here. We will find other accommodations for our Sunday services. Perhaps if we find a new gathering place, they will follow us there."

"What about Chloe? Isn't she here, too?" Regan asked.

"She never was. She was an innocent child who moved to the next plane as soon as we said the guiding prayers she needed."

Practitioner Fitzwater closed his eyes and resumed his unintelligible chant. Regan and Tom took it as their cue to leave.

As soon as they were far enough down Empire Grade to pick up a cell signal, Regan called Dave. His answering machine picked up; he wasn't at his desk. She was so anxious to tell him about her new data and explain her theory of how Paul and Hector had been murdered by their own hand that she raged at the machine in frustration.

"Of course you're not in! Why are you never in when I have something important to tell you?"

"Cause if I was at your beck and call every time you had another crazy idea, I'd never get any work done. Which is why, when I saw your phone number, I let you go to my answering machine," Dave replied in a tone of voice as agitated as hers. "Last time I made time to see you, you walked out on me. Remember?"

"Last time I only had a theory. This time Tom's with me and we have convincing evidence."

"Tom's in on this with you? Why didn't you say so? In that case, come by my office in half an hour. Oh, and Regan, I missed lunch so I'm real hungry. Could you bring me a snack?"

She imagined him grinning mischievously as he waited for her to launch into a feminist tirade about professional women still being treated like waitresses so she ignored his poke and parried with, "Sure. Just have some of that wonderful police coffee ready when we get there. I like extra cream in mine."

They brought Dave goodies from Zoccoli's Deli, a downtown Santa Cruz institution. Dave reneged on his part of the bargain, instead directing Tom to the break room when they arrived.

Regan didn't wait for Tom's return; she was too impatient to sit quietly.

"Dave, look at these and tell me what you see." She handed her collection of Taylor and Christopher printouts to him.

"I see your little tree-hugger and her green-haired buddy get their picture taken a lot."

"Notice anything about Christopher in the pictures?"

"Yeah. He must keep hair dye companies in business. He doesn't have the same hair color in any of these. This his latest look?" Dave held up the conventional brown-haired picture of Christopher.

"It is."

"I guess he decided it isn't easy being green."

Dave was still chuckling at his Kermit the Frog reference when Tom returned clutching a steaming paper cup in each hand. "What do you think?" he asked as he gave Regan her coffee and sat down.

"Thank you," she smiled up at Tom. "Dave thinks he's much wittier than he really is," she said before Dave could say anything, "and he hasn't yet figured out the rainbow connection." Regan's smile said she appreciated her own Muppet cleverness as much as Dave appreciated his, "So you haven't missed anything."

Dave studied the printouts again.

"See. His hair is always a different color. Over time, he's had hair every shade of the rainbow. El Arco Iris: the rainbow man. Hector wasn't the rainbow man the FBI is looking for, Christopher Smith is."

"We spoke with Practitioner Fitzwater," Tom added, "Hector and Christopher knew one another. They were both members of Fitzwater's group for a time before the Practitioner tossed Christopher out, pronouncing him as unfit to be a member."

"Christopher was Hector's connection in the business," Regan explained, "and not as Special Agent Gibbons likes to say, 'Just his little local grower connection.' As unlikely as it may seem, I was right about seeing him at Paul's on the night of the FBI bust. He was there with the smugglers. He must have escaped into the woods during the sweep and had a fall or brush with a branch as he fled because he had a cut over his eyebrow the next time I saw him, which, by the way, is still there. He's trying to hide it with makeup."

"His colorful hair is gone now," Tom said. "Taylor Bingham told Regan that was because Christopher wanted us to know he was going to be a stable tenant when we rented Paul's house to him, but we think he's doing his best to look different than he did as the rainbow man."

Dave nodded, just his head at first and with reservation as he pondered what Regan and Tom said, but finally with enough enthusiasm that he rocked forward and backward on his chair. "I'll pass this on to Special Agent Gibbons along with a strong suggestion that he reconsider who El Arco Iris is."

"There's more, Dave, Regan knows how Paul was made to commit suicide."

Dave cocked his head and stared at her wordlessly.

"That's right."

"Your ghost again?"

"No. We all know Paul didn't see a ghost. He, however, thought he did. He always felt guilty for the death of his daughter. Either out of desperation, because traditional medical treatment was failing to save her, or because he was as much of a true believer in the Practitioner and his Prayers as Hector was, he let Hector convince him to go into a marijuana growing partnership to fund prayers for Chloe.

"The only thing was that in his mind he didn't act quickly enough to save her and he blamed himself for that and thought he caused her death."

Regan tried to be careful about how she explained Melody's connection even though she thought Dave would understand. "When Melody found out what was going on, she demanded that Paul stop growing. She thought he had ..."

"You're trying to say Melody was never part of Hector's little co-op, aren't you? Or at least that's the story you're pussy-footing around with, hoping I'll miss her role in this business. I'm smarter than that, Regan. And I've had too much experience in the way criminal behavior works to let you get away with that.

"Not only that, I'm real disappointed you think you can

shade the truth to me, or that you think you should. That doesn't speak very highly of the kind of friendship I thought we had."

Tom cast a sideways look at his wife. She couldn't have appeared to be in more pain if Dave had physically slapped her.

"Please don't think I wanted ... please, Dave, I never ..." she stuttered. "Yes, I've been trying to keep Melody's real involvement out of all of this. She appealed to me as a mother; she asked what I would have done in her place to try to save one of my children. I would have done exactly what she did, which was to agree to the growing scheme. To her it was a way to pay for one more chance, one final try to cure her daughter.

"As soon as Chloe died, she did tell Paul to quit. He told her he had, but he hadn't. Melody never profited from growing marijuana. Now she's pregnant and after all she's been through with losing Chloe, I couldn't put her future at risk. She doesn't deserve jail time for what she did, Dave.

"I couldn't tell you what I knew about her involvement, but it had nothing to do with what I think of your intellect or abilities. I didn't want to put you in the difficult position of having knowledge of a crime without reporting it, because that's what I would have asked of you.

"We are good friends; I should have trusted you and let you decide for yourself how to handle the Melody problem. I'm so sorry I didn't."

The rims of her eyes filled with tears as she spoke. She blinked quickly, trying to keep any from escaping and running down her cheek.

Dave sighed and was quiet for what to Regan seemed like hours.

"Apology accepted," he said finally. "And I'm good with secrets, especially ones that uphold the spirit of the law rather than the letter of it." He added quickly, "That's a comment that's not to leave this room, by the way.

"So can you go ahead and tell me how the not-ghost convinced Paul to kill himself now or do we have to all join hands and sing a few stanzas of *Kumbaya* first?"

Tom was thankful for Dave's quick forgiveness, but not nearly as much as Regan was. She sniffed and made a pass at her eyes this time, using fingertips to keep her tear-dampened mascara from being smudged.

"No singing, please; I've heard you two guys sing. I don't deserve that much cruel and unusual punishment."

"Then let's hear what you got," Dave pressed.

"We know Christopher is the rainbow man and Hector's connection."

"Likely is the rainbow man and probably Hector's connection," Dave corrected.

She knew, even if he wasn't sure. She went on, ignoring Dave's qualifier. "Paul's suicide was premeditated murder. Hector told me that he had been getting nocturnal 'visits' from Chloe, or at least her voice. I believe Paul was having the same experience. It wouldn't have been that hard to broadcast a voice into the house …"

"Wouldn't Paul recognize his own daughter's voice?" Dave played devil's advocate.

"I don't think so. Melody told me she found it quite troubling that she was losing her memory of what her daughter sounded like. If she was, Paul was, too. If a little girlish voice spoke to him about something he already felt guilty about — and again, Hector said Paul blamed himself for not going to the Practitioner soon enough — and especially if the voice woke him up in the middle of the night and accused him of not trying hard enough to save her life, I believe his guilt would make him accept that the voice he heard was Chloe."

Dave bobbed his head. "For the sake of your story, OK, let's say Paul thought he was hearing his daughter."

"I think the plan was, that on the night Paul committed suicide, Christopher and his 'little girl' accomplice were going to tell Paul what they told him in the woods …"

"Which was?"

"That she was lonely and lost and needed a parent to come to her and that if her daddy wouldn't, she'd take her mommy. I told you that before, but you just made a joke about it. Don't you dare do that again, Dave."

Dave leaned back in his chair.

"That's what Hector said he heard the child say. Their divorce-in-progress was Melody's idea, not Paul's. I've heard it from a number of people that he wanted her back because he still loved her. That threat was real to him. He traded his life for hers.

"Hector's turning up at Paul's that night was just an inconvenience in the planned murder-made-to-look-like-suicide, but Paul chasing Hector through the woods fits and even reinforces another part of the story.

"Hector said Paul caught him rifling through his belongings. Hector said he was looking for money, but Paul thought he was trying to steal evidence: the evidence that Paul had about the woman ring leader. You know what I think?"

"Tell me."

"I think Paul and Melody really did want out after Chloe died, but they had signed incriminating documents just like Tom and I did. I think Paul managed to get some equally incriminating evidence against Christopher and the woman running the operation and was using it as blackmail to get them to let Melody out of the business."

"You think the woman and Christopher still had Melody's signed contract and promised to keep it locked away if Paul still let them use the property and kept what he had against them a secret, too? You think it was kinda a quid-pro-quo blackmail thing goin' on?"

"Exactly. Paul's house was ransacked after he died. My guess is whoever did that was looking for Paul's evidence and didn't find it."

Tom added, "That's probably what the rock-throwing people on our hillside were looking for."

Dave didn't have a comeback. His only reaction was puffing his cheeks out with air and releasing it in a pop. "Wow. So, what happened next?"

"Hector ran. Paul gave chase, firing at him as they ran. Paul must have had his handgun with him, too. Perhaps he planned to get up close and personal with the smaller gun and scare Hector ..."

"Wouldn't Hector have been scared enough what with Paul trying to shoot him?"

"No. He said Paul was a good shot and wasn't trying to

kill him or he would have. At some point Hector stopped running, too — we know that because they got into a shouting match outside our house — and as Hector said, if Paul wanted to kill him, he could have then."

"That still doesn't explain Paul's suicide."

"The original plan was to have a costumed and made-up Chloe visit Paul at home. Plans got changed, but only a little. The 'ghost' had to run after Hector and Paul, but she could have because she was fit and knew how to move in the woods. When she caught up with them, Christopher backlit her with a flashlight and Taylor made her speech ..."

"Taylor? Taylor Bingham? Not her again. You had me going there, Regan, but not Taylor Bingham again."

"Why not? She's tiny like a child. Her voice — have you listened to her? When she's not being strident, when she's trying to side with you and get her way, she has a sweet little girl sound. And unless you think somehow Paul was made to come to the precise spot in the woods where his killer was waiting, or better yet, that the real spirit of his dead daughter materialized on the spot and spoke to him, who better than Taylor Bingham to have been up to a chase through the forest?"

"It follows, too, Dave," Tom said, "that if Christopher Smith is the rainbow man and he's a co-operator with a woman, it's likely that the woman is Taylor Bingham. Nothing happens in her woods that she doesn't know about; it doesn't seem possible growing and importing could take place under her nose without her knowing about it, let alone one run by an associate of hers."

"If I agree with you about your tree-huggers ghosting Paul

to death-by-dead-daughter, what about Hector? How'd they get him?"

"I'm not sure about him. He did say Chloe had visited him, at least her voice had, and that she told him Paul was angry at him for letting them linger without prayers. At first Hector said he feared they might come for him like Chloe had for her father, but he said the last time she spoke to him, Chloe told him Paul had forgiven him.

"Hector begged me to sign the paper he gave me because he said he had already been paid an advance for Tom and me signing on, and that he'd given his advance to Practitioner Fitzwater for prayers. I guess Taylor and Christopher, whom Hector genuinely feared, by the way, could have threatened him with exposure to the Practitioner. Hector worshipped the Practitioner and didn't want him to know what he did for a living, but," Regan shook her head, "I just don't think Hector would have chosen suicide over being outed, so there has to be something more going on. I just don't know what it is, yet."

Dave sat still, definitely in pondering mode. "Okay. So you have a theory — and I admit one that even though it's kinda wonky is sorta' growing on me — and some photos that argue Christopher Smith could be El Arco Iris." Dave tipped his head from side to side.

"Now, that may be enough to get Special Agent Gibbons to pick up Christopher and sweat him a little, maybe even put him in a lineup and see if the El Arco Iris name-dropping Colombian is willing to recognize him — which is unlikely if the guy doesn't want to wind up somewhere with his tongue cut out — but the thing is, unless the formerly green-haired

Christopher flips on your little tree-hugging pal — which is also not likely for all the same reasons the Colombian won't point him out — we got nothin' on her.

"And don't forget, Taylor Bingham has her reputation as queen of the woods to fall back on. She's gonna' swear on a stack of Bibles made from non-old-growth-paper-pulp that she would never, never, mess with any people who might in any way mess with her foresty tree-friends. You see the problem we have?"

"I do, Dave," Regan replied.

"So how do we get around it?"

"By taking one small step at a time," Tom said.

"Could I ask a favor, Dave?" Regan asked.

"What kind of favor do you want this time?"

"Could you hold off on bringing Special Agent Gibbons in on this until we have some hard evidence?"

"Leaving Special Agent Gibbons out of this for the time being wouldn't be a favor, it would be a relief."

Tom poked his head into Regan's office on his way to the back parking lot, "We're on for 6:15," he said. "See you later."

Regan wandered up to the reception desk and gave Amanda a note. "This is a reminder — not that I expect you need one — but here's one anyway. Call my cell phone at 6:23, precisely."

Amanda beamed. "Yes ma'am!" She looked left and right quickly and dropped her voice to a whisper, "I'm so excited, I've never been part of a sting before."

As arranged, the office was empty and the front door locked when a triumphant Taylor walked through the back door trailing her Christopher. She sailed past Regan's open office door with eyes straight ahead and turned left into Tom's office. The greeting pleasantries Regan could hear were her cue to begin their plan. She pocketed her cell phone, and began slowly counting to one-hundred in her head. As she counted, she switched on the tiny recorder on her desk and pressed the button on her office phone that opened the intercom to Tom's office. When she reached her silent one-hundred, she quietly closed the door to her office, and walked across the hall to join them.

Christopher jumped up and stood when he saw her in an over-the-top gesture of politeness.

"Sit down, Christopher. Please."

He flopped back down in a slouch next to Taylor on the sofa where Tom had placed them.

Regan read the smiles that greeted her: Taylor's was victorious, Christopher's obsequious, and Tom's indicative of a man genuinely enjoying his game.

Taylor spoke first. "Regan, your husband tells us you have finally seen what an opportunity you have in Christopher."

"Have I?" She directed a look at her husband designed to demonstrate displeasure with him. "Tom thinks we can come to terms for Christopher's tenancy, that's clear."

"I think Regan's remaining concerns center on the rental duration and the amount of compensation we'd be receiving."

"All details we can work out," Taylor said happily.

"How long do you think you'll be our tenant?" Tom asked.

Christopher opened his mouth, but as usual Taylor spoke for him as if he weren't in the room. "Christopher is a good student, but he's changed his major recently so he has at least two more years of undergraduate work. Then he'll probably want to do graduate work, isn't that right, Christopher?"

"Um, yes …"

"So, we'd say he'll be in the house for the foreseeable future."

Both Taylor and Christopher offered unctuous smiles.

"Fine, fine," Tom said, "so we're looking at a long-term agreement. Now about the rent ..."

"We understand how difficult the rental situation is in the Santa Cruz area," Taylor commiserated, "especially so near UCSC" — Christopher nodded his newly crop-cut and brown-haired head vigorously — "and he is prepared to pay whatever you think is an appropriate rent."

It was Regan's turn to smile. "We think if Christopher is going to become our tenant, we need to reconsider our other contract first."

Taylor looked puzzled, Christopher's stare was blank, and right on cue, Regan's phone rang.

She pulled the phone out of her pocket and looked at the screen. "Sorry, I need to take this. Excuse me," she said as she left Tom's office.

"Thanks, Amanda. Your timing was perfect. Now I have to say goodbye and be very quiet."

Regan opened the door to her office carefully, stepped inside, and quickly and quietly closed it. She leaned against the closed door as if ready to prevent any intrusion. Tom's intercom was working perfectly; she could hear every word being said and so could the recorder.

"I don't see the need to play games," Tom spoke, "we're all friends here, some of us more than others, but Regan's out of the room," he joked. "We three all have the same interest in mind, which is to help one another make money."

"That may be your primary interest; mine is to save our woodlands," Taylor delivered her stump speech.

"Of course, it is and we all know how having the

reassurance that you can do so without any complications is so helpful, and that having Christopher rent our house will go a long way to ensuring that."

"I'm perplexed. What are you suggesting, Tom?"

"I'm a real estate broker. I live by contracts and I want to be clear that any contracts we all agree to are mutually satisfactory. Let me give you an example of what I mean. I'll say 'we' for the sake of making my explanation clear.

"Now suppose we signed a contract spelling out what percentage of profits I was to receive from our business venture. Suppose I signed in good faith only to discover later that you hadn't disclosed the full extent of the income-producing opportunities my property was offering to our joint venture. Naturally, when this was pointed out to you, you would be uncomfortable — probably quite embarrassed at your oversight — and want to redo our contract so that it accurately reflected our mutual expectations."

Regan reopened her office door, left, and carefully closed the door behind her before she made her way back to the conversation unfolding in Tom's office.

"Have we agreed to a redo of our contract?" Regan asked. "Tom, I hope you and Taylor — and Christopher, too — have because I'm unwilling to sign Christopher up as our tenant until that matter has been settled."

"All this talk of contracts has me bewildered. I thought we were here to talk about Christopher," Taylor gibbered.

"It's quite simple, Taylor, either you agree to new terms for the use of our land or we'll have to seriously consider renting to someone else."

Taylor's eyes narrowed and she seemed to regain her

composure. "I don't know what you mean; I have no idea what you're talking about, Regan."

"That nice young officer who has just moved here from Tennessee and was recently hired by the Santa Cruz Police Department is looking for a rental. That was him on my phone. His references are as impressive as your vouching for Christopher."

"Is he the officer who came to our house the night Paul committed suicide?" Tom asked.

"He is. I believe he's still involved in the Paul Valentine investigation and I bet he's going to be on the investigating team for Hector Gonzales, too, since both deaths are related."

Christopher blurted out, "Why would the police care about those suicides? It's not like they were murder or anything like that."

"Why do you think Hector's death was a suicide, Christopher?" Regan asked.

Taylor quickly put a hand on his arm. She raised her other hand motioning for him to be still before she formed it into a fist with her index finger extended and pressed the finger to her lips in the universally recognized sign for silence.

"I'm afraid there is some sort of misunderstanding between us," she said. "Christopher and I have no idea what you're talking about. We are here to set the terms for his renting your house. It doesn't seem like that's what you want to discuss so I see no need to continue our meeting. We'll come back when you're ready to talk about renting to him."

As they passed her Regan said, "Better yet, why don't you let us know when we're on the same page and are ready to talk about Christopher's tenancy. Just don't wait too long or we'll have to rent to that police officer. If we do, Taylor, you may run into him on one of your hikes; I understand he's a curious man who enjoys long walks in the woods."

Regan and Tom lived in suspended animation until they heard the back office door click closed. Regan still hardly breathed as they opened her office door and stopped the recorder. When she heard a car drive past her office on its way to Swift Street, she was finally willing to make noise. Her first audible sound was nervous laughter.

She flung herself into Tom's arms. "What do you think; how'd we do?"

"We should know soon," he said before he kissed her.

🏠🏠🏠🏠🏠🏠🏠🏠🏠🏠🏠

The revised contract arrived like the first one had: pushed through the front door mail slot in the middle of the night in a sealed envelope addressed to Tom. Amanda dutifully gave the envelope to him like she had the first one, only this time she breathed a little faster than normal and said knowingly, "It's here," as she delivered it.

It was a copy of the original documents signed by Regan and Tom with revised phraseology. The limiting phrase, "marijuana growing" had been crossed out and replaced by "all" and after "for the production, processing, and distribution of recreational cannabis," the words, "and imported products," had been added. As the document now read, they were promised fifty percent of all profits their property produced. Implied in that was that they were now to be co-equal partners in any future drug smuggling.

"Do you think it's enough?" Regan asked after she read the contracts.

"Coupled with the tape and your El Arco Iris research, it seems to me like it is. Let's go drop our evidence off with Dave."

After a good twenty-four hours had passed without an update from Dave, Regan began calling him. She tried several times, but it was late the next day before she succeeded in reaching him. Dave answered with a business-like, "Officer Everett."

"Dave, have you been avoiding me?" Regan asked. "I had to call the main desk, give a false name, and ask them to connect me with whoever handled animal cruelty complaints to get through to you."

"Yeah, well I've seen your messages, but I've been busy."

"No, you haven't. You've been dodging my calls."

He exhaled loudly. "You ever heard the term 'mindfulness'?" Dave asked.

"Sure," Regan replied.

"Well Special Agent Gibbons listened to your tape, read the revised contract you got the next day, took a look at the pictures of your rainbow-haired dude, and said he was gonna' have his people keep an eye on him, but for the time being not alert your green-haired pal to the fact that he may be in trouble. I call his approach 'mindfulness policing.'"

"I call it disappointing," Regan snapped.

"See, I knew you'd get all worked up when I told you. Which is why I didn't."

"What more does he need? No one other than Hector, who's dead, us, and the people on the other end of it know about our contract. Taylor wants Christopher installed in the house. We say we won't do that unless and until we get a better deal with our land use partners, and amazingly we get a revised contract with the changes we wanted the day after we discussed them with Taylor and Christopher. And we got the discussion on tape for good measure. How is that tight little circle of events not enough for Special Agent Gibbons?"

"I'm not sayin' it isn't; I'm sayin' what you got is still circumstantial and Special Agent Gibbons is still out there fishing, using your green-haired guy without him knowing it, and hoping by watching him he can hook that big shark he likes to metaphorize about so much. Give it time, Regan, and keep playing along with your formerly green-haired guy."

"What about Taylor?"

"What about her?"

"What did Special Agent Gibbons think about her as the mystery woman? More importantly, Dave, what did he say about her being instrumental in Paul's suicide and probably causing Hector's, too?"

"He didn't have anything to say about her. She was cagey on the tape, you know."

"But what about her playing Chloe's ghost?"

"We didn't talk about that."

"You didn't tell him about that, did you?"

"If I had, you would have heard Special Agent Gibbons

laughing all the way to Bonny Doon."

"Hector told me ..."

"Hector's dead, remember? Without him to say, 'Yeah, I saw it,' what he told you he saw becomes hearsay. Wild hearsay. And the part about him thinkin' the little ghost girl talked to him is not only hearsay, it gets written off as a nightmare. Without Hector, no one saw what your little tree-hugging buddy did, and she's not going to turn herself in, is she?"

"I think Christopher saw her; I think he helped her. Hector said Chloe appeared suddenly in a cloud of light. My guess is Christopher manned the lights; he'd be a surviving witness."

"If he had any motivation for talking, which he doesn't, what's he gonna' say, anyway? 'We punked the guy and he shot himself and we decided to do it again to see if it was a fluke, but dang, the second guy did it, too?' I'm not sure impersonating a ghost is a crime, and if I'm not sure, you can be darned sure some defense attorney is gonna make sure a jury isn't sure either."

"Taylor finally left happy," Regan said to Tom. "I preferred it when she stomped out of my office angry or frustrated, or both. But now that we've agreed to let Christopher rent the house, they feel they have the upper hand."

"It's only a temporary victory for them. Focus on that."

"I intend to do more than think positively. As soon as he's settled, I'm going to bake him some chocolate chip cookies, take them to him as a little housewarming gift, gossip a bit, and see if I rattle his cozy relationship with Taylor. Nothing will improve my mood more than sowing a little dissention in the ranks."

🏠🏠🏠🏠🏠🏠🏠🏠🏠🏠🏠

Regan was knocking on Christopher's door three days later, a beach-themed canister of chocolate chip cookies in hand.

He had installed a peephole — without permission, she noted — and she was so certain he was looking at her through it that she plastered a big smile on her face and waved while she waited for the door to open.

Christopher only opened the door wide enough to peer out. It was after noon, but he looked sleepy and like she had awakened him.

"May I come in? I have cookies."

"Cookies?" he said enthusiastically. "Yeah, come in."

His eyes never left the container as she walked it to the kitchen. The greedy way he studied it suggested he had recently sampled some locally-grown produce.

"I see you haven't quite finished settling in," Regan said, noticing the many boxes still to be emptied.

"Yeah. I've been pretty busy." He opened the cookie container and helped himself to one. "OMG these are so good. Would you like one?"

"No thank you. I just wanted to see how you like the little house."

"I like it a lot." He helped himself to another cookie.

"You haven't seen any ghosts, have you?" Regan asked lightheartedly.

"No ghosts. There aren't any ghosts here."

"Are you sure? Hector told me he saw the ghost of Chloe Valentine the night her father died."

Christopher giggled and reached for another cookie.

"But I guess you know that's not true."

"Yeah," he chuckled.

"Do you own a gun, Christopher?"

"Me? No."

"Well, that's good, at least."

"Why? What do you mean?"

"We both know Paul and Hector didn't see a real ghost, because, like you said, there are no ghosts here, but they both thought they did and it troubled them so much that they used a gun to take their own life. Since you don't have a gun, you can't be coerced into doing the same thing. So that's good."

"I don't have a guilty conscience either, not like those guys had. I mean like they must have had."

Regan laughed lightly. "Of course you don't, so you have nothing to worry about from ghosts, real or impersonated. Still if I were you, I'd lock my door at night."

"Why should I do that? These are the best cookies I've ever had, by the way."

"If I were you, I'd lock my door, not because I was worried about a spirit getting into my house, but because, as the only other person who knows there weren't any ghosts around when Paul and Hector died, I'd be a loose end."

"I…," he frowned, "what do you mean?"

"I mean you're the only one who can tie Taylor Bingham to the deaths of Paul Valentine and Hector Gonzalez, and, if I were you, I'd be more than a little nervous about that."

Regan waved her hand in front of her face. "What am I saying? You and Taylor have a long, close history and have worked together for years, right? She values you, of course she does. As I see it, she would never wish you any harm … unless she thought you might break your confidence with her, tell tales about her. Ask her, I'm sure she'll agree."

"I don't talk or tell tales."

"Then you have nothing to worry about. I'm glad you like it here, Christopher. Enjoy the cookies, and remember I'm right up the hill if you ever want to talk or need anything."

🏠🏠🏠🏠🏠🏠🏠🏠🏠🏠🏠

"Is this Regan McHenry?"

The voice was familiar, but even though Regan prided herself on never forgetting a voice, she couldn't quite place it.

"Yes."

"It's Christopher. Christopher Smith." His voice was muffled, muted, like he was trying not to be overheard. "I could use some help."

"What sort of help do you need, Christopher?"

"I need you to come and get me."

"Where are you?"

There was a long pause before he answered. "I'm in the FBI field office in Palo Alto."

"What are you doing there?"

"I'll tell you on the way home."

"Would you like me to call Taylor and see if she can come get you instead?"

"No!" he sounded alarmed at the suggestion. "Please. Don't let Taylor know I've been picked up by the FBI."

He gave her the address and she told him she should be there in about an hour.


The check-in procedure at the FBI field office promised to be as complicated as getting behind the security doors at the Santa Cruz Police Department, but she didn't have to go through the whole process because she was intercepted by Special Agent Gibbons who vouched for her.

"You're the one Smith called? Interesting. You must have a lot of aptitude for getting people to trust you. So here's what you do: you go pick him up and give him a ride home. Keep playing along and letting him involve you even more. Don't push too hard or take chances — remember I'm the one who does the heavy lifting."

"I'm curious, how did he wind up here?" Regan asked.

"I thought it was time Mr. Smith had a little sweating and some very public alone time with the law. I've found nothing makes a businessman more nervous than thinking his boss will find out he's been spending one-on-one time with the enemy. And if the boss does find out — hoooo-whee!" he whistled through a laugh.

"But Dave said you weren't going to do anything about Christopher except watch him."

"Like most police, your friend's a competent foot soldier, but he's no general. This isn't a battle we're trying to win, it's a war. What we're trying to do here is above his pay grade — yours, too, except you aren't getting paid," he laughed, enjoying his joke immensely — "so I don't feel the need to fill him in on the FBI's every move."

He took her hand in his, but this time when he grasped it for a handshake, he used a firm but gentle grip. "Thanks for your help; it's great to have you on the team."

Regan wondered if she'd been too quick to dismiss him as nothing but a blowhard the first time she met him. Today he had his ego dialed back and was working her like a consummate pro. He'd probably worked Christopher as well.

Christopher hooked his arm through hers so she could

guide him and walked to her car with his jacket over his head. He kept his head down and covered long after they drove out of the parking lot and until they were far from the FBI office.

"You said you'd tell me what's going on if I collected you," Regan said as he surfaced. "I'm doing that. Tell me what happened."

"I got picked up and put in a lineup. All of us had to wear green wigs. That Gibbons guy kept telling me I'd been ID'ed by a drug smuggler, but I know he was making stuff up."

"I'm surprised you called me instead of Taylor. Why did you do that?"

"I don't want her to know about any of this. Even though I wasn't charged with anything, just being picked up looks bad. It's important to her that I never get arrested for anything but the environmental cause. Besides, she has a rule: no talking to anyone without her in the room.

"Being hauled in like this might make her mad at me even if there's no reason why she should be. I can't take the chance, not with Taylor. Besides, you said to let you know if I needed anything."

Christopher remained silent for the rest of the ride back to Santa Cruz. After a few attempts, she gave up trying to engage him in conversation, but she peeked at him every once in a while. He wasn't disinterested in talking to her; he had other thoughts on his mind. He looked frightened and not just about Taylor thinking he had sullied the environmental cause.

As she dropped him off at the rental house, he skipped a thank you and said instead, "I've been thinking about what you said about loose ends, but see, I'm not a blabbermouth so nobody has anything to worry about with me."

🏠🏠🏠🏠🏠🏠🏠🏠🏠🏠🏠

"This is an FYI call just so you can't say I never tell you anything," Dave said when Regan answered their home phone. "Course you would have heard about it in a few minutes when the nightly news starts, but I thought you deserved a heads-up."

"I'm listening; sounds important."

"More like ironic. That formerly green-haired guy renting your house was found dead ..."

Regan's head swirled and she thought she might throw up.

"... looks like when he was outside your rental doing a little cleanup after that big windstorm we had last night, a tree limb fell and knocked him on the head. 'Tree-hugger killed by a tree' is the headline they'll probably use. Like I said, ironic, don't you think?

"Regan? Regan, did you hear what I said?"

She heard but she couldn't speak.

"Regan?"

When she did finally answer him, Regan's voice was devoid of emotion. "She killed him, Dave. Taylor Bingham killed him."

"I don't think so," he chortled. "She'd have to be some serious kind of tree whisperer to do that. She'd have to get the dead guy to stand in exactly the right place and then convince a big tree branch to drop on him while he was there. No. It was an accident, pure and simple. You've had too many people die around you in too short a space of time. It's messin' with your head. Talk to Tom, have a glass of wine, and let it go, Regan."

When Tom came home, Regan was flipping from station to station trying to catch every word being spoken about the unusual accident that killed Christopher Smith.

"Dave called and said you were pretty upset ..."

"This is Taylor's doing. She didn't want Christopher implicating her in the drug business or in Paul or Hector's deaths so she killed him." She spoke rapidly, picking up speed with each word.

"Sweetheart, you're taking a big leap here imagining Taylor's behind ... behind ... well ... everything that's happened lately. I'll give you she's the woman in the drug operation." He shook his head, "Although proving it isn't possible right now.

"And Paul and Hector? We both believe she manipulated Paul," he said with certainty, "and may have — but only may have — done the same thing to Hector, but there's nothing to tie her to Christopher's death. The timing is odd, I agree, but his death truly looks accidental."

"How can you say that?"

"Simple: I reached that conclusion from what Dave told me about the physical evidence. If someone tampered with the branch, marks would have remained on it — saw marks or rope marks from tugging — and there were none. If the branch was dropped, it would have come straight down, needle side away from the tree.

"But if it was compromised by all the wind we had and still remained attached, it would have partially collapsed at an angle against the tree so when it finally broke free, it would have fallen straight down next to the trunk, needles first, bounced, and landed with the densest part of the branch swinging over away from the trunk.

"The branch on Christopher's remains was positioned like it would have been if it had a gradually detaching fall with needles near the tree and the business end of the branch on Christopher's head. The physics involved argue for an accident."

Tom was right. She'd seen the redwoods near them drop branches and watched hired tree trimmers work; in both instances the branches fell as he said.

"It's just such a coincidence — I mean the timing and the fact that he was afraid of what she'd do if she found out he'd been interrogated by the FBI — it's hard not to imagine ..."

Regan took a deep breath and exhaled slowly. "You and Dave are probably right. I'm seeing connections where there aren't any; next I'll be seeing ghosts.

"The news says he was found by a friend, but didn't name names. Did Dave say who found him?"

Tom hesitated. He knew how Regan would take it when he told her who found Christopher. "Taylor Bingham."

Wednesday dawned clear and bright. Regan planned to use her day off to water plants and take comfort from the late spring abundance of flowers in her garden. She moved from plant to plant, shutting off the water after she finished with one and bending over to carefully place the nozzle at the base of the next plant before she turned it on again. It was a tedious and mindless task, just what she needed to rest her body and soul.

She didn't notice her company at first. The visitor's shadow was low because of the height of the sun and the person casting it was behind her, so she felt the presence of Taylor Bingham before she saw her.

Regan stood immediately to make herself as large as possible, the same thing she'd been told do in the presence of a mountain lion.

Taylor's stance was her usual slightly confrontational one: feet splayed, one hand on her hip and the other grasping her sturdy walking stick which was poked into the ground and held upright at a slight angle, but the smile on her face was as warm a one as Regan had ever seen her produce.

"I'm pleased to see you using your time well, taking care of these living things while judiciously saving our water resources."

"I'm pleased you approve of my watering; your approval is so important to me." Regan forced sarcasm into each word she spoke.

Taylor appeared to not notice. "What happened to Christopher is such a tragedy, but the living must move forward; he'd be the first to say so. In that spirit, I have a new tenant for your little house. He's also involved with nature, and while I haven't had a long association with him, I have great confidence in his future and can vouch for him wholeheartedly."

Regan should have been taken aback by Taylor's audacity, but nothing the woman said moved her any longer. Her question was sharp but her delivery was measured. "Is he an environmentalist or a pot grower, or both?"

Taylor threw her hip-hand up over her chest, "Regan, you never cease to amaze me, the things you say to me …"

"Or is he someone who will help you the next time you want to do a neighborly little killing?"

The elfin Taylor stood stock-still, her smile frozen. Her expression changed to anger so slowly Regan felt like she was watching a child's game of red-light-green-light: movement was taking place, but it couldn't be seen it until it was upon her.

"I've had just about enough of you and your innuendos."

"Then let me say it clearly, Taylor. You've been running a drug operation in Bonny Doon and you convinced Paul Valentine you were his dead daughter and demanded he take his life to protect his wife. You did something similar to Hector Gonzalez, and, I don't know how you did it, but you killed Christopher Smith, too."

Taylor smiled again, more a bared-teeth expression than a toothy grin. "It wasn't that hard. I eased him near some trees as we talked and walked, then I used my walking stick to kill him. I dragged a convenient, properly sized branch over him to mask my blow and then used another branch to wipe away any drag marks. You should know that I took no pleasure in doing what had to be done. His death was strictly business.

"Oh, don't eye my walking stick, I've already used bleach to clean any traces of blood off of it." She chuckled with genuine pleasure.

"Hector was easy, as well. Christopher and I took him into the woods and gave him a choice: he could kill himself quickly with one bullet or we would kill him slowly with many. He chose the easy way out."

"Hector was harmless."

"He was a weak link, the only one who could connect us with Paul's suicide and the only one who would dare identify Christopher as being his connection in the drug business.

"I hoped with Hector gone that would be the end of it, but even without him, Christopher became a liability." Taylor shrugged. "Such a shame. I warned Christopher after he spoke so openly with Hector at the little Valentine girl's memorial and I thought he learned. He learned nothing.

"Do you know the morning I killed him, when we went for what was to be one of our usual pleasant walks, he blurted out that he'd been picked up by the FBI and that he'd called you for a ride home so I wouldn't know? He couldn't even keep his mouth shut about that. I had to take action. It was just a matter of time before he gave me up.

"He'll be blamed for the drug operation, but without him to involve me, that's as far as it will go. A copy of that silly contract Hector had you and your husband sign will be found among his possessions: the cherry on top of an ice cream sundae.

"I'm going to take a time-out, something I do periodically when the authorities get too close, and redouble my environmental efforts, so it will look like he was indeed behind everything and acting alone.

"So now you know everything," Taylor giggled like a little girl. "I'm going to enjoy watching how you manage your complete knowledge without ever being able to prove any of it.

"You have a lot to think about; why don't I give you a week before you meet your new tenant?"

Taylor turned to leave, took a couple of steps, and turned back. "Oh, and not to threaten you — I wouldn't want to do that — here's something else for you to think about: I know where you and your husband live. And since you put all the pieces together so cleverly, you know what I'm capable of."

🏠🏠🏠🏠🏠🏠🏠🏠🏠🏠🏠

Tom had heard it all before, so as they sat in Dave's office and Regan reiterated what had happened in her garden to Dave and Special Agent Gibbons, his reaction was calmer than Dave's, but still not as blasé as the FBI's finest.

"So, you blame the Bingham woman for three so-called murders, murders which have been officially ruled two suicides and an accidental death," Special Agent Gibbons outlined what Regan had said. "And you have no way of tying her to the drug operation ..."

"What do you mean? She told me! Isn't my word as good as hers?"

"You want my honest opinion?"

"Yes, of course."

"OK then, no, it's not. I know how you and your husband have tried to help us out, but if I didn't know you, and you told me this cockamamie story about ghost impersonations and faked suicides and murders, I'd think you were a little touched.

"Add to that, that real estate agents rank below used car salesmen in the public eye when it comes to being honest and trustworthy, and put you up against a 'Woman of the Year' award winner with a long list of environmental savior awards, whose attorney will say she would never do anything to damage her precious forest land — and marijuana grows do that — and who do you think a jury would believe?"

Dave couldn't be silent any longer. "She threatened Regan and Tom; didn't you hear that part? This is a woman who operates with Colombian drug smugglers and has killed people. Are you saying she gets a pass? Tell me that's not where you're going with this!"

"Come on, Officer Everett, you understand how the legal system works almost as well as I do. You know no prosecutor is going to go to court with what we've got."

"Then get more," Dave shouted. "Regan and Tom are my

friends. From where I sit, they're in danger. You can't ignore that."

Special Agent Gibbons held up his hand in his now familiar traffic cop style to stop Dave's outburst. Regan began to think that was the only thing he did well.

"That's exactly what we're going to do. It will take some time, especially if she goes to ground, but we'll keep an eye on her. Eventually she'll make a mistake."

Tom entered the conversation with deadly calm. "That is if I don't shoot her first."

"Now, Tom," Dave tried to soothe his friend, "don't go saying things like that."

Tom's wrath should have been directed at Special Agent Gibbons or at the unfairness of the situation, but instead he aimed it squarely at Dave. "She's threatened me and my wife. You may sit by and wait for some terrible outcome, but I intend to protect Regan and myself, as well."

"Calm down, Mr. Kiley," Special Agent Gibbons commanded. "Nothing's going to happen to you or your wife. If the Bingham woman was intent on harm, she could have done something to Regan when they were alone in the garden.

"From what you say, there's real animosity between Regan and her. She said she was going to enjoy Regan's torment; I believe her. She knows by now Regan's told others what she said. She has nothing to gain by harming either of you and a lot to lose if she does because if anything were to happen to either of you — even an accident of some sort — no one in law enforcement would rest until we connected her to your deaths."

Regan rolled her eyes, "Well, that makes me feel better."

After Special Agent Gibbons left, Dave offered his own recommendation. "Tom, just so you understand, I didn't say don't get a gun, and I didn't say don't use it if you need to protect yourself and Regan. All I'm saying is don't say that's your plan in front of an idiot like our favorite special agent.

"And don't worry too much. Much as I hate to agree with him, I think he's right, but if he's not, you still don't have to worry because us lowly locals will have your back for as long as it takes."

Regan sat at her computer entering photos and a description of what she was offering on *Craigslist*. As she typed, she had a serious talk with herself about the future.

*You can start at every sound, see lurking figures and danger everywhere, or you can get on with your life and not give Taylor any satisfaction.*

She chose the last option. "You hear me, Sophie and Harry," she spoke to her cats who were sitting nearby ready to become her typing assistants, "Taylor isn't going to ruin my life."

She verbalized her decision as if that would give her thoughts greater weight. It was a good plan for handling fear; handling the lack of justice for Taylor was another matter altogether.

Regan finished the entry and put it in the 'free' section, wondering if she should post the giant table and chairs Paul Valentine built to shelter his horses under 'furniture' or 'farm & garden' as well.

The phone rang within twenty minutes of her posting.

"Yeah, Hi, I saw your ad," a man's voice said. "Is that the table and chairs in Bonny Doon?"

"The same," she said.

"I've seen them," he sounded enthusiastic, "we go by them on our way to get our Christmas tree every year. Free, huh?"

"All you have to do is take them down and away."

"Yeah, I can do that; my brother's got a big hauling truck. Me and him can come by on Saturday, say about 10:00?"

"That will be fine."

"Here's my number," he read out several digits, "you give me a call if you give it to somebody else before I get there."

"It's yours, I promise. See you on Saturday."

🏠🏠🏠🏠🏠🏠🏠🏠🏠🏠🏠

Tom volunteered to oversee the removal of the table and chairs, pleased that once they were gone the threat of litigation with the County would go away, too, and they could get clear title to Paul Valentine's property. Regan planned to skip the removal, but by two in the afternoon her curiosity got the better of her and she made the short drive to watch.

The *Craigslisters* had disassembled the wooden structures — they had plans for the wood, not for the composition as it was — and were putting the final pieces in their truck when she arrived.

"We'll take the decorations if you want," they offered, pointing to the folded checkered tablecloth and brightly colored wooden flowers in their blue ceramic pot that had topped the table, "unless you have a use for them."

"They're yours," Tom said.

"Umm, I'll take the flowers and the pot," Regan said quickly. "I'll put them in my garden." She smiled at Tom, "I can't think of a better way to symbolically flip off Taylor."

"Want me to put them in your car?" the *Craigslister* asked.

"Would you?" Regan replied.

He bent to pick up the pot, but it was heavier than he expected. He stumbled under the weight of lifting it and it fell on its side, spilling colorful wooden flowers on the ground.

"Let me help you, "Tom offered.

Regan began picking up the flowers as Tom and the man carried the pot to her car. In the midst of the spilled flowers she discovered a sealed plastic bag inside a small glass jar. She picked it up and inspected it.

"Tom, look at this," she held it out toward him, a frown on her forehead. "It was in the flowerpot. What do you think it is?"

He opened the jar and then the bag and dumped a small key out into his hand. There was still something inside the bag. He reached back inside and pulled out a folded piece of paper.

Regan leaned against him as he unfolded the paper; they read a handwritten note at the same time.

*If you find this key, it means something has happened to me. The key is to a safe deposit box at Wells Fargo Bank on River Street in Santa Cruz held under the name of Pablo Valentino. Give it to the police.*

"I understand they're picking up Taylor Bingham as we speak, or rather drink," Dave said, holding his glass aloft.

Regan clinked her champagne glass against his and then did the same with his wife, Sandy, and finally with Tom. "Do you think they'll get her for murder, too?" she asked.

"Doubtful," Dave answered. "Remember Valentine's confession implicating her as his partner was written before she started killing anyone, but it outlines an ironclad case against her for drug running.

"Your Paul Valentine was one clever guy," Dave said. "He must have figured his house, car, everything he owned could be searched by the bad guys, but who would think to look for a stash in a big old flowerpot?

"If he wanted to move his evidence, all he needed to do was take the key out of the flowerpot, and if something happened to him, eventually someone would take down that table — maybe a new owner like you guys wanting to clear things up with the County — and his baggie would get found.

"Your dead neighbor was thorough, too, keeping that payment ledger initialed by both of them every time they got paid and split the money. You know what I like best, though? I like that tape he made talking to your little tree hugger about how careful he and Hector were going to be with their growing so they wouldn't hurt her woodlands and her saying that was almost as important to her as the money was.

"And getting a couple of bank employees to act as witnesses and sign their names over the seal on the package

255

and then watch him put it in his safe deposit box was genius. So, no murder charges right now, but she's going away for a long time.

"Hey, do you think she'll lose some of her awards? Didn't Bill Cosby get some of his honorary degrees rescinded when the scandal broke about what he did to those women? That would ruin her day big time," Dave chuckled.

"That might be worse for her than prison," Tom agreed.

Regan had grown pensive as they celebrated. "Melody and James are in Scotland being married. She said they want to look for a beach house getaway when they get back; that's the future business she was talking about when she delivered my Clan Buchanan chairs. When I see her, should I tell her what really happened to Paul?"

"I would," Sandy said. "It might be hard for her to hear initially, but don't you think she deserves to know what her first husband did for her?"

"You're right," Regan nodded. "After some tears, she should feel well loved."

"You owe it to Paul even more than to her. Our dead neighbor should be remembered for the complex man he was. He hurt some people, true, but he gave everything for those he loved," Tom said.

"You guys are getting so maudlin and sentimental," Dave said, "I almost forgot to ask. That young cop from Tennessee — you remember him from the first night when this started, don't you?"

Regan nodded.

"He's experiencing sticker shock with rentals in Santa Cruz and he's got a big German Shepherd named Harley, so house hunting is even harder. He asked me to ask you if you'd be willing to rent the little house to him and his dog. He'll put the fake floor back in the sentinel house and cover up where those drug runners stashed stuff, if you want, or leave it open for a wine cellar, if you don't, and having a cop and a well-trained dog on your land couldn't hurt. What do you say?"

"Done," Tom barely waited for Dave to finish his sentence. He grinned at his wife. "You didn't know Regan threatened Taylor Bingham with just such an arrangement to force better terms out of her for our drug dealings."

🏠🏠🏠🏠🏠🏠🏠🏠🏠🏠🏠

That night was the first since Paul Valentine died outside their house that Regan slept well, undisturbed by the haunting echoes of his cry before he took his life. She hoped that meant he and Chloe, and even Hector, had moved on to the next plane that they and Practitioner Fitzwater believed awaited them, and were finally at peace.

About the author

Nancy Lynn Jarvis finally acknowledged she was having too much fun writing to ever sell another house, so she let her license lapse in May of 2013, after her twenty-fifth anniversary in real estate.

After earning a BA in behavioral science from San Jose State University, she worked in the advertising department of the *San Jose Mercury News*. A move to Santa Cruz meant a new job as a librarian and later a stint as the business manager for Shakespeare/Santa Cruz at UCSC.

She invites you to take a peek into the real estate world through the stories that form the backdrop of her Regan McHenry mysteries. Real estate details and ideas come from Nancy's own experiences.

For small presses, getting exposure in the marketplace dominated by big publishers is a challenge, but it is also one where you as a reader can help us enormously by spreading the word.

So, if you have enjoyed this book, please help us to promote it and other Good Read Publishers and Good Read Mysteries titles.

There's a wide range of ways you can do so, including:

- Recommending the book to your friends
- Posting a review on Amazon or other book websites like Goodreads
- Reviewing it on your blog
- Tweeting about it and giving a link to our website at http://www.nancylynnjarvis.com
- Suggesting the book to your book club
- Posting a comment on your Facebook page
- Liking our Facebook page at http://www.facebook.com/ReganMcHenryRealEstateMysteries?ref=ts
- Pinning it at Pinterest
- Anything else that you think of!

Many thanks for your help — it's much appreciated.

At http://www.nancylynnjarvis.com you can:

- Read the first chapter of the books in the Regan McHenry Mystery Series.

- Review reader comments and email your own.

- Ask Nancy questions about her books and the next book in the series.

- Find out about upcoming events, book club discounts, and arrange for Nancy to talk to your book club or group.

- Read or print Regan's recipe for the chocolate chip cookie dough that she and Tom always have ready in their freezer.

Books are also available in large print and for your Kindle, iPad, and other e-readers.

www.ingramcontent.com/pod-product-compliance
Lightning Source LLC
Chambersburg PA
CBHW050020180626
46810CB00002B/507